The HarpIES

T.S.Nicholl

ISBN: 1999730909
ISBN-13: 978-1999730901

DEDICATION

To Debbie.

CONTENTS

A T.S.NICHOLL PUBLISHING PAPERBACK

The HarpIES
First Published in Great Britain 2017
Copyright © 2017 T.S.Nicholl

1 THE MORNING AFTER

Gerard Moran woke with a start at the alarm. He must have fallen asleep, but did not remember doing so. In fact, he didn't remember getting back home at all. Before him there was only the horror of yesterday afternoon, then it was darkness, and the next moment a July morning sun streamed in through the flat's windows as though nothing was wrong with the world.

His eyes followed the clock on the bedside cabinet, blankly watching but not registering the hands of the dial tick around its face. He tried to settle on a thought, a mind's-eye image of anything that would allow him the pretense these stalking memories were just cobwebs of a foul dream. But his mind wouldn't afford him the luxury, and stubbornly continued to bludgeon onwards with its internal stuttering jump-looped film reel.

Sitting up, Gerard waited for his throbbing head to slow its spinning before rising unsteadily from the bed. He followed his normal routine, and walked across the room to the en-suite and turned on the shower. Autonomously he stripped off the bloodied jeans and t-shirt he found he still wore; absently noting he'd been sick on himself at some point. Gerard's head pounded, the inside of his skull scraped raw as though something nasty had recently gnawed its way out. He felt a thick jagged pressure which stabbed at his mind with every movement. Entwined in this was the ever increasing stack of memory pressing on memory, from which he couldn`t find release.

Stepping in under the shower's flow, Gerard hoped the water would somehow wash away the scrambled thoughts. But as the pressured stream hit him, something akin to a flaming metal shard ripped its way through his temple. He staggered backwards, almost cracking the sides of the glass cubicle as he rattled off them in his retreat. Instinctively he turned away from the main force of the shower, fumbling with the handle of the sliding panel. The misted glass and plastic slipped under his grip, while his head screamed in escalating white noise. Gerard's mouth opened to echo the internal sirens, an unnatural howl escaping from him. With a final brute strength effort wrought from the pain, he wrenched the door aside and fell outwards onto the cold tile floor.

Immediately a dark aura tried to wrap itself around him, grasping and dragging his consciousness back down into the silent darkness. Gerard involuntary retched, but there was nothing left inside to throw up. His entire being was empty and battered, while over it all still lorded the white-hot needle which incessantly bored through his mind. Even before realising it himself Gerard's jarred emotions over-ran his limited mental defences, and consumed in the memories of the last twenty-four hours he began to sob uncontrollably.

*   *   *

Mandy, Gerard's girlfriend of a long-standing six weeks was supposed to have met him after finishing work. She had a job in her dad's generic 'Coffee Bean' franchise on the concourse at Manchester's Piccadilly train station, but had fallen ill on her shift and went straight to his flat instead.

It didn't take Gerard long to get back to the rented one bedroom apartment in the city centre, but Mandy had already gone to bed. He checked in on her, and even with the most cursory of unskilled looks he was worried by her condition. There was a grey, almost bloodless pallor to her skin, and she was shivering but had a burning high temperature. Her chills escalated to fever level within minutes of his arrival, and by the time a panicked Gerard phoned the emergency services he could feel the heat perceptively radiating out from her.

Although it seemed an age the ambulance arrived only a short time later, but already Mandy's pain had reached the point where she couldn't stand anything touching her, even the sheets she lay on. It was all too much as the medics tried to ease her onto a stretcher, and she emitted one final blood-chilling scream before thankfully falling unconscious. Gerard knew unconsciousness was never a good thing, but it had to be better than the tortured screams and escalating pain, which seemingly the medics could do nothing to ease.

Mandy came around again towards the end of the journey to the hospital, and for a moment she seemed lucid. However, no sooner had they thought she was levelling out when convulsions forcefully set in. Red speckled foam and spit bubbled from her mouth, as she jerked and shook while Gerard impotently looked on. The paramedic tried to keep her still, but she thrashed around wildly and only remained on the stretcher as she'd been strapped in for her journey down from the flat. For a second all activity ceased, and then Mandy re-opened her eyes. Gerard gasped in horror at the dark red filled orbs staring back. Her normally clear blue eyes had changed to fractured marbles, which looked as though every blood vessel in them had exploded.

Mandy renewed her struggles again, violently now, and with purpose. She stretched up and sunk her teeth heavily into the medic's exposed arm as he knelt over her, biting deep into the flesh. The ambulance man screamed in agony, and staggered backwards clasping at the wound as blood poured from it. Mandy continued to pull at the straps, trying to free herself, all the while garbled guttural noises rose from her like the rage of an injured caged beast.

Somewhere in the background Gerard heard the driver shouting, then moments later the ambulance turned and braked sharply. The medic was propelled down the vehicle and took Gerard with him, both of them crashing into the doored partition that separated the driver's cabin from the back of the ambulance. The rear doors swung open immediately, revealing staff from the hospital who were already waiting. Gerard started to untangle himself from the medic, still unable to take his eyes from Mandy. In little more than an hour she had changed from a sick girlfriend, to this rabid animal thing. He barely noticed someone was talking to him.

"Sir, can you hear me? Are you injured?" Gerard looked at the man as though he spoke in some unknown tongue, the shock of what was happening around him setting in.

"No...No, not me - him." He said absently, talking about the medic as he continued to watch the staff try to safely remove Mandy from the ambulance.

"Sir...Sir!" Gerard could feel himself being shaken, and tried to focus on the person before him. "The woman you're with, where's she been today?"

"The station, she was working at the train station - Piccadilly. What the hell's happening to her?" Notes of panic creeping into his monotone responses.

"She's another from the station - Isolation two now." The doctor shouted at those battling to keep her on the bed, ignoring Gerard's questions

Gerard found himself being pulled along by the arm, dragged through to an already busy emergency room behind the trolley that barely held Mandy in her continued struggles.

"What's happening? Where are you taking her?" He pulled his arm from the doctor's grasp, now demanding answers in his ascending panic.

"Sir, we've..."

The doctor didn't get time to finish the sentence. Even over the din of the emergency room, you could hear crashing and then screams behind the swinging double doors where Mandy had just been wheeled. As though in anticipation the room quietened, then the same doors burst open and a nurse bundled out with the front of her uniform awash in red. She fell to the floor, shaking in a fit as she clutched at her neck, which jetted blood. The doors swung shut, but instantly crashed back open. Gerard's stomach turned as another figure lurched into view - it was a blood covered Mandy who was finally free of her restraints.

People quickly backed away from the scene, creating a vacuum around Mandy and the nurse. Two flak-vested policemen, who had been talking to the reception staff stepped into the void, and raised their semi-automatic weapons as they did so.

"Armed Police! Down on the ground!" One of the officers shouted, but other than turn Mandy's attention from the nurse to the officer this had no effect.

"Stay where you are! Get down on the ground!" The officer shouted again, but she still paid no attention and stalked slowly forward as though gauging their reactions.

The officer looked like he was about to speak again, but the forgotten nurse had silently risen from the floor, and with a garbled scream ran at the officer closest to her. She attacked him in frenzy, biting at his face and neck, blood spraying everywhere as both of them fell in a tangled mess to the floor. Mandy took this as her cue, and launched herself at the remaining policeman. Then one of their guns went off, and pandemonium broke out in the frozen crowd around them.

People began screaming and pushing each other, trying to get to away from the flash point. Those too slow or sick were pushed aside, or trampled underfoot as mob mentality broke out in the room. Gerard tried to stay his ground, but the flow of fear was too strong for him. There was no choice other than be swept along with the crowd, and even then he was just able to keep his footing in the stampede heading for the exit.

Just before the door Gerard managed to turn around, and for a second saw Mandy again. She was on the ground now, a dark red slick expanding out from her still body on the white tiled floor. A blood soaked officer stood with his gun trained on her, and then they were both lost from view as the crush of bodies filled in behind him.

2 THE NIGHT BEFORE

Gerard found himself outside the hospital, milling around the entrance doors with the others who'd managed to flee the emergency room. No one could get back in again, or see what was happening as the external doors locked automatically and no reachable windows had a clear view inside.

The police 'Tactical Aid Unit's' couldn't have been far away, as they arrived within minutes of the exodus from A&E. One of their two white vans, emblazoned with a yellow and blue `Armed Response` on the side screeched to a halt in the ambulance bay, while the other disappeared around the side of the building. Four black jumpsuits exited from the sliding side door of the remaining van, leaving the driver and passenger to hang back at the vehicle liaising with their base. Immediately they began clearing the front of the hospital, with a single mandate - Get people out of the area. No questions, no messing about, and there wasn't going to be any kind of debate.

"This accident and emergency department is closed. If you need to see a doctor urgently, additional resources have been allocated at the Manchester Royal Infirmary on Grafton Street. Please move away from the area as quickly and orderly as possible."

The barking dismissal came from one of the van front occupants, who had just produced a loud hailer, his message leaving little room for interpretation. Anyone who didn't start to move began to be accosted, and only those who looked like they could expire immediately were left alone.

Gerard didn't know what to do. The cops didn't care about anyone's story, never mind weighing up the merits of allowing individuals to stay or get back inside. The few hospital staff who could be found were already overwhelmed by helping those in most need, and the general public was as clueless as him. All Gerard could think to do was ring Mandy's parents. He didn't know how to begin and tell them what had happened, but aimlessly standing around was not an option.

Gerard brought out his mobile and rang their number. The home phone was engaged, but he had no other to try. He rang again, and then a third time, praying someone would hear the 'Call Waiting' tone and pick up. The same busy signal eventually beeped back at him each time, but at least someone was home. Their house was less than a half mile from the hospital, and with no better plan Gerard set off running in that direction.

It didn't take him long to get to where Mandy's parents lived. Arriving at the top of their street he was more than relieved to see their car parked outside, and ran flat out for the final distance.

"Look at this guy!" Gerard passed a footpath wide break in the middle of the house row, where a small group of people hung out drinking on the corner, trying to wring the last out from the summer's day.

"Fuck me, look at the blood on him!" A different voice to the first rang out, but Gerard neither heard nor saw either of them, his focus completely on the house.

Reaching the front door, he opened it without knocking. The lock rested on its latch, as it always did when someone was at home.

"Hello? Jeff, Ellen - its Gerard!" He shouted walking into the hallway.

There was noise coming from the TV in the living room to his left, and Gerard opened the frosted glass paneled door to go in. Immediately he could see something was wrong, as the normally immaculate living room didn't look its usual self. Two of the seats around the family dining table had been knocked over, and what looked like the takings from the coffee shop lay strewn over both the table and floor. The telephone was sounding its disconnected tones, as the handset had been knocked from the cradle. All of which led to ornaments smashed around the fireplace, and a trail of pieces leading through the room like breadcrumbs. Looking around Gerard slowly walked through, his sense of foreboding continuing to rise as a sound from the kitchen attracted him.

"Jeff? Ellen?"

He saw Jeff's feet first, lying prone on the floor, randomly twitching. The rest of his body came into view as Gerard moved across the open plan room toward the kitchen.

"Jeff?"

Jeff was face down on the kitchen lino, his body sprawled outwards facing towards the back door. Ellen had attacked him from the behind, and she was still straddled on his back with a thick dark blood pool slowly expanding around them. Gerard's enquiring voice had distracted her, and she looked at him over her shoulder with the same dark red eyes he'd seen on Mandy. Her face was dripping in blood, as she absently chewed a piece of flesh like it was bubblegum.

The thing that had once been Mandy's mum turned as she got to her feet, moving towards Gerard in a single fluid motion. Too frightened to do anything else, his instinct immediately made him back away and try to keep as much distance and furniture between them as possible. Ellen mirrored him step for step, until Gerard bumped a side table knocking over one of the many ornaments that peppered the room. The slight distraction acted like a starting pistol, and she lunged towards him but there was too much in her way to make contact. Gerard didn't wait for her to force the next opportunity, and made a break for the hallway.

Running back through the open hall door, he slammed it behind him. Ellen collided with the glass screen moments after, shattering the large etched pane and covering them both in broken shards. Gerard didn't stop moving, and backed away from the door as he watched Ellen shred herself on the broken glass forcefully squirming her way through after him. Knowing she wasn't going to stop, he kept on and ran out the open front door, but collided with another person coming in. His momentum carried him onwards, and stumbling a few steps he finally fell onto the flat green canvas of the front garden.

"What the fuck are you doing?" Gerard looked up at a glowering thirty-something tattooed skinhead, who unknown to him had been part of the drinking group he'd passed.

There was no chance for explanation, as from within the house an animal like screech escaped, and suddenly Ellen appeared in the doorway sprinting toward them. Gerard cowered, waiting for the impact, but she ignored him and leapt screaming at the larger newcomer, both of them tumbling onto the grass. The skinhead shouted to his friends as he struggled to protect himself against the ferocity of the wild attack. Ellen tore at his face and body with her nails, all the while trying to bite him. Another member of the group ran over, and there was a sickening crunch sound as a boot connected with Ellen's face. The force of the blow snapped her head back, and she fell unmoving onto the lawn.

"What the fuck was that about?!" The skinhead shouted at Gerard as he got up and dusted himself off, wincing at the rising angry looking welts when he touched his face. The skinhead's anger flared further after noticing his companions sniggering and mimicking his recent cries for help. Not waiting for Gerard to answer, the thickset aggressor stomped the few steps over to him and connected a heavy punch on his jaw.

Gerard didn't hear anything after, or even see the hulking shadow bear down upon him with disgust on his face. His head had struck one of the pointed kerbing stones that marked out the path along the front garden, and everything beyond that impact was black. The group left him bleeding where he was, and walked toward the house. Barely conscious, Gerard eventually got up and staggered off into the night. Somehow he made it back to the flat on autopilot.

3 FAMILY MATTERS

Gerard was beginning to feel the cold. The drying water from the shower, and normally welcoming cool of the bathroom tiles had crept up through his bones as he lay hunkered on the floor. He felt little difference after his big emotional release. The old wives tale of 'crying it all out' was just that for him - a tale. If anything, he now only felt slightly embarrassed about his naked and teary state on the bathroom floor.

Shivering on the tiles a moment longer, he slowly picked himself up and got back into the shower. The exercise now was as much to raise his temperature as anything else, and this time he made sure not to put his injured head in the way of the powered jets.

After finishing he used the magnified shaving mirror above the sink to get a closer inspection of his varying injuries. Initial impressions were far from positive. A result not helped by growing up on a small island just off the north coast of Ireland, which provided him with a grey skin pallet as inheritance. Last night's stress, with the additional head trauma kicker had turned him an almost ashen colour. Sunken dark ringed eyes provided an additional indicator that yesterday had not been one of his best, but the main problem was a large discoloured lump just at his right temple. This lump was almost volcanically crowned with a slightly bleeding rectangular hole in its middle, about a centimetre in diameter.

Gerard tenderly touched the beaten face staring back from the mirror. If the reflection had been a photograph, you could have easily convinced him the dark brown eyes staring back belonged to a stranger. Then he remembered Mandy's eyes, and her mums – crazed and inhuman.

"Stop it!" He shouted at the mirror, trying to cut off his spiralling train of thought.

He could feel his heart hammering, trying to break out through the rib cage. The blood rush of endorphins beginning to overwhelm his brain. Gerard breathed deep, trying to settle himself. He put his hands on his head in anxious movement, and accidentally touched the angry wound on his temple. Again it was a visual jumble of violence, teeth and blood, so much blood everywhere.

"Stop it!" He shouted at the mirror again. "Come on Moran, stop it. Practical, think practical… Clothes, get some clothes on."

Gerard went back to the bedroom to redress. His headache hadn't improved from the bathroom visit, but at least he still didn't feel his brain was about to blow apart. His train of thought spiraled to retrace yesterday again, and he cursed himself in hindsight with the things he could've done differently. The result would have been the same no matter what his actions, but that didn't stop him feeling a coward for leaving Mandy, a deserter in her hour of need. Running off to her parent's house had been stupid and selfish move. Panic got the better of him, and that was the simple truth. He'd wanted to dump the responsibility of Mandy back onto her parents, only to find they were in worse shape than anyone. Now, even if just for the sake of his own conscience he had to go back to the hospital and find out what happened, then do the same at the house.

Nursing his head Gerard walked to the kitchen and took a bottle of headache tablets from a drawer under the sink. He stared out the small window, down the five floors to ground while trying to swallow a couple of the chalky pills. From his lofty vantage of the flat everything seemed normal, but it was difficult to tell. This was Sunday morning, and at the moment only litter moved in the shuttered streets.

He returned to the front room, and sat down on the sofa to think, automatically flicking on the TV. There was no intention to watch, but the news was on and he recognised the photograph in the background as the station at Piccadilly. The report began to show CCTV footage from the area, and inset into the video was a grainy photo of a middle-aged man. Gerard turned the volume up as the male announcer continued.

"…authorities are still trying to locate Dr. Nathan Harper, a geneticist at the St. Mary's facility in Manchester, and lecturer at the local University. Yesterday the BBC, and a number of other media outlets, received a 'self-described' manifesto detailing the release of

the IES virus in the vicinity, and possibly other locations. Some of this morning's tabloids have already coined this as 'Harper's IES' or 'The HarpIES' virus. At present we are unable to provide any specifics concerning the contents of the document, but the following statement was made by the Health Protection Agency earlier this morning."

The screen flickered for a moment, then a figure appeared, fortyish, slightly balding, grim faced and tired looking. He stood behind a podium displaying the HPA crest, and beside him as though part of a supporting cast were a few recognisable members of parliament, including the Prime Minister, some military types in uniform and other serious looking men in suits. Gerard was surprised the spokesman wasn't from the government, but clearing his throat the man behind the podium started a nervous sounding speech.

"Since approximately 3pm yesterday, the Health Protection Agency and conjoining authorities have been tracking an escalating health issue within the UK. At this point we have confirmation from the St. Mary's genetic research facility in Manchester that initial symptoms relate to a variant of a virus known as Intracellular Endocrine Syndrome, or IES. Samples of the mutated virus have been found in both air and surface content around the Piccadilly station area.

At this time we advise all members of the public to be vigilant. The variant is in a highly contagious form, and current reports indicate the mutation has been re-engineered to target the female population. Contact with the virus in its airborne form can have an incubation period of around three hours before symptoms become fully apparent, although fluid exchange with an IES host can result in an almost instant reaction. Any members of the public who display flu like symptoms which escalate within the hour, or those who believe they have been in contact with an IES host, please contact one of the below numbers immediately. Teams from the Health Protection Agency hotlines are waiting for your call. We have been directly liaising with local health authorities and emergency services to coordinate..."

Gerard didn't know how long he'd heard the music in his peripheral hearing, before the brain registered his mobile was ringing in the bedroom. Rushing to find the phone, he got up and stumbled into the next room where the noise came from. Immediately Gerard's head began to pound even harder, with only the small exertion. He found the phone in the pocket of his blood splattered jeans, still ringing. The name on the screen read *Motty* - his brother.

"Alright ball-bag." Dermott's mocking thick Irish accent initiated the conversation with one of his regular openers. "How're the English bastards treating you?"

"Fucking hell Motty, not today. Something's really wrong here." Gerard replied. He didn't want to say the words, but knew there would be no choice eventually. "I think Mandy's dead."

The line was silent for a moment, before the reply came back.

"Ahh piss off. You nearly had me there you crazy bastard. Jesus, that's a bit dark for you innit?"

"It's true, turn on the fuckin' TV! I was there, she was...and her parents..." The random words spilled from Gerard in a torrent. He could feel his brain trying to click back into panic mode just by talking about it, so he abruptly stopped speaking.

"Holy shit!" The voice came back, either finally registering Gerard wasn't joking or he'd just turned on the TV and saw things for himself. "What the hell's going on?"

Difficult as it was Gerard went through a brief coverage of the last twenty-four hours, part by staggered part, all the while trying to keep his roller coasting emotions in check. Dermott stayed silent as the story unfolded, at least until Gerard mentioned he was going back to the hospital again today.

"Go back, are you fuckin' mad!?" He butted in. "That place is still going to be locked down, guaranteed, especially if people are being taken there to be treated. Anyway, suppose you do go back. What are you going to tell them that they don't already know? If you think you need to do something, then ring one of those numbers and..."

Gerard felt the concussion from the explosion before he heard the blast. The building shook in the shockwave, and he was surprised the windows didn't shatter as he watched them bubble inwards with the pressure. The lights in the room flickered for a moment, and then they and the TV blew out together. A multitude of alarm bells began ringing in the buildings around him, and looking out the nearest window he could see a thick plume of smoke rising from the direction of the university. He only remembered Dermott was on the other end of the telephone, when tinny shouts could be heard from the forgotten mobile in his hand.

"I'm here, I'm here." Gerard spoke into the phone, surprisingly calm, still staring out the window at the rising smoke. "Something's just blown up, something big by the look of it. I can't see much from here, but there's loads of smoke."

"Jesus Christ G. Fuck that place." Dermott replied. "You need to leave now, and get your arse home. Ring whoever you need to on your way back to Rathlin. I'll even pick you up in the boat if it'll get you out of that shit-hole."

At any other time Gerard would have thought Dermott was just trying to get him back to the island again for his own selfish reasons. Every opportunity since Gerard told Motty he intended to travel for a while, the "when will you be back" conversation came up. The whole trip was only supposed to be for a couple of months, and he would have probably returned to Rathlin already if he hadn't met Mandy. His Manchester stop should have been for a few days, but eight weeks later and he was still there. Until yesterday his only real concerns were the depleting savings in his account, but things had definitely changed now.

"I need to sort this Mandy thing out first. I'll ring you later and tell you what's happening." Gerard came back, still determined to try and redeem himself first.

The line was silent for a moment, before Dermott responded.

"You do what you need to mate. Just be safe, and don't take long about it. Make sure you ring me tonight. I want you out of there soon as, even if I have to drag you away myself."

Gerard could tell Motty wanted to argue the point about leaving, but each brother was as hard headed as the other. Motty knew until Gerard was ready, he'd only be wasting his breath trying to convincing him otherwise.

The conversation ended with Dermott making Gerard again promise to ring him later. Gerard continued to stand by the window watching the black plume of smoke spread across the sky. It was a dark bruise on an otherwise clear blue day, and seemed to be getting thicker and heavier by the moment. His brain ran through a dozen scenarios. Paranoia told him these events had to be related, as there was too much happening for it all to be coincidence. Still he couldn't let it rule him and needed more information to confirm things one way or another. He wanted to ring the helpline and offload his lot, but without electricity there was no way to get the numbers from the TV. He had no choice but to go out and deal with things in person. It was the only way to be sure.

4 FURTHER CONCERNS

Gerard prepared to leave the flat. Normally this would've meant little more than ensuring his keys and wallet were with him, but today there was no telling what could happen and he'd always been a bit of a boy scout. His intention was only to go to the hospital, and try to speak to someone about Mandy and her parents. Still, with everything being an unknown he grabbed a backpack regularly used around town, threw in a bottle of water, a couple of chocolate bars, the multi-tool and lights for his bike, and a thin but heavy wooden rolling pin the previous residents had left hanging from a hook inside the front door - just in case. Last night showed him that sometimes you needed a 'just in case' handy.

Ensuring the door was secured behind him, Gerard left the flat. Straight away his resolve was tested, for as soon as the door closed he was instantly plunged into an echoing gloom. He stood for a moment while his eyes got used to the dim of the hall. There was a small window at the opposite end of the corridor to the emergency exit, but its dirty glass wouldn't allow through enough light for anything other than shadows. Gerard went to his bag, and fumbled around for the front bicycle light so he could see the way before him. He felt a little more confident with the beam clearing away the darkened corners, and quickly walked the hall to the emergency exit door and stairs.

He descended the empty, echoing stairwell with caution. The comfort of his light now a necessity, as the emergency lights were out and without it he would be completely blind. He burst out into the daylight on the ground floor, breathing a sigh of relief as the sun touched him. The moment quickly left though, as immediately a noticeable acrid smell assaulted his nose. The air was like the morning after bonfire night, a heavy, almost tangible substance, tinged with sour undernotes. Alarm bells still rang in the background, and now he was outside Gerard could make out the mingling sirens of fire crews and ambulances. Whatever caused the explosion, it had enough impact to send the emergency services out in force and this did nothing to improve his confidence.

Although the noise and smells sent Gerard's apprehension spiraling up, he didn't let them send him scurrying back inside. Instead he walked around the building to the resident's storage, where each flat had its own small lockable container built into the ground floor. He kept a bicycle used for transport around the city here, and walked the bike back through the resident's car park noticing an unoccupied car with its boot open. The vehicle was already half filled with hastily packed belongings, and waiting for its final loads from the absent owner.

Pressing the barrier button that separated the private car park from the general population, Gerard walked under the rising arm and waited until it closed behind him again before moving off. With a quick look up and down the empty street, he set towards the direction of the rising smoke. He turned onto Market Street, the main retail area of the city centre. Even though it was early on a Sunday morning and an explosion had just gone off within walking distance, people still shopped as though it was a regular day. All the businesses had their doors open, even if staff from some of the smaller stores were standing outside smoking and talking, while they cast worried glances in the direction he was going.

Leaving them behind Gerard kept cycling toward the smoke. As he got closer, the damage from the explosion became more and more apparent. The smell of burning overrode everything now, while the smashed windows quickly increased in frequency. This was the case until he turned onto the long straight road of Deansgate, which ran passed the courts and down to the University. Before him, but still a good distance from where the smoke was rising, he could see a fluttering cordon stretched across the road. He was surprised the area was already sealed off as it was less than half an hour since the blast, and he rode to where a small crowd gathered. Two uniformed Policemen walked the line to keep onlookers from going any further. Gerard stopped beside a small group of bag laden middle-aged women who were talking among themselves.

"Anyone know what's happening?" Gerard asked the group as a whole, hoping one of them would break off from their conversation and reply.

A short, slightly overweight woman, who was well into her late forties turned to answer him. She hesitated a moment, noting his broad Northern Irish accent and battered appearance. Chances were it wasn't beyond her memory when the IRA still visited Manchester and other English cities with their own explosions and coded warnings. Back in the 80's and before, Gerard would have already been wrestled to the ground and arrested for being in the same city where random explosions were going off. But things were different in the wake of 9/11, and a new stereotype of terrorist nestled in the public's psyche. The woman left her childhood hang-ups where they were; seemingly enjoying the fact she could share a few choice titbits with someone less knowledgeable than herself.

"We heard it was a bomb." The lady spoke, dropping her volume of speech as though letting him in on the secret. "This is the second cordon." She pointed down the road. "The first is way down there, near the university."

Gerard looked, but could see nothing at this distance. A grey and black haze hung in the air, but barring the broken windows, a lack of people, and a few police cars with their lights flashing the street looked the same as ever.

"A bomb! Jesus." Was all he could think to say, and hoped the woman would feel like elaborating further.

"Yeah, so he was saying." She replied, nodding over to a man who stood at the side of the road, and was animatedly talking to anyone who'd listen. "He said they were already evacuating houses when the explosion happened. Supposedly people were passing out in the smoke, so they pushed the cordon back here. I've not seen them myself, but they were sending in people with yellow plastic suits and helmets to the university."

Gerard had a good idea what suits she was talking about, though he'd only ever seen them in films or the TV where some catastrophe had just happened - biological protection suits. That realization settled any lingering doubts as to his next move. For once he was going to take Motty's advice, and leave for Rathlin as soon as he could.

5 RETURN TO THE SCENE

The cordon quickly filled with new watchers and enquirers, so Gerard left them to the rumour mill. His decision to deal with the 'Mandy and parents' situation hadn't changed, but wheeling his bike away from the line he couldn't shake off the sickening feeling that something else was about to happen at any moment. He needed to finish in Manchester and get away from the city.

Even though his head pounded heavily, he decided to leave the hospital visit to last. On a normal day you could wait for hours to be seen at any A&E in Manchester, and guaranteed this waiting time would have stretched to infinity after the earlier explosion, and the previous day's events - if they were letting people near at all. To get to the hospital from his current location would mean passing near to Jeff and Ellen's house anyway, and a re-visit there might help to fill in the blank spots from last night.

Decision made, Gerard moved off. He hoped by the time his business was finished at the house he would be able to make a more informed decision about where to go next. In the meantime, there was little choice but to cross his fingers and hope things didn't get any worse. It would be difficult enough to get passage home at present, and another incident may tip the balance altogether. Even though it hadn't been reported on the news, he could only assume Manchester's airport would be closed along with the local train stations and bus depots where the infection began. If this were the case it would mean travelling an extra hour or so to Liverpool, to try and get a plane or ferry to Ireland from there. The problem with that choice was anyone in the North West of England would be thinking along the same lines, and any public transport that was still running would undoubtedly be swamped. A smarter, but even longer journey would take him to Stranraer, or its close neighbor of Cairnryan in Scotland. If transport in England was stopped altogether, then Scotland would be the logical place for Dermott to pick him up. Either way he'd only have time to go to one of the two places, so his choice needed to be the right one.

Setting aside the final destination, Gerard turned his attention back to current transport problems. It would be difficult going anywhere of distance with the bike, and he'd never even thought about getting a car for the city. If he was honest he'd never bothered applying for a driving licence. Most of the time there was little police presence on Rathlin, especially those on the prowl for locals committing minor traffic violations. Usually all you had to do was not crash into anyone, or thing, and no questions were asked. There was no doubt it would definitely be easier with a car, and there was only one place he knew where to get one without having to steal it. Fortunately he was going there already - Mandy's parents.

Keeping to the quieter back streets, Gerard returned to the housing estate where Mandy's parent's lived. Images from the previous day kept trying to force themselves on him - Mandy's dad, half eaten on the kitchen floor, or her mum blood covered and manic. Those damn red eyes following him everywhere. For all he knew Ellen could still be lying in her front garden, or out attacking random innocents. He prayed no matter how things ended, that someone had the decency to call the emergency services. He already had more than his fill of death for the near future, and didn't know how he'd react to yesterday's horror spilling over into this new day, especially when it was those he knew.

Involuntarily he stopped his bike at the top of the road. It was as though some invisible force held him while hammering at his heart. Hot sweats rose up through him, as he reacted to being back so soon. Every fibre screamed to turn around and leave, and he wanted to, but couldn't, not until he knew for definite what went on.

Taking a deep breath Gerard pushed off again, with a growing feeling of being watched. It didn't help that the normally busy street was unusually quiet, empty in fact. While the road wasn't a hive of activity all the time, on the occasions he'd been there it had never been deserted. This was a July Sunday morning, and there wasn't a kid playing out or even a dog barking. Something was definitely amiss, and as he got closer to the house at least part of the reason came to him. Not only was the scene unusually quiet, but Mandy's parent's car was missing from the front as well.

Leaving his bike on the garden path Gerard walked up to the front door, trying to suppress the ever-increasing desire to turn around and run. Looking around for signs of last night's activity he could see some blood on the paving stones and grass, but little else to show anything out of the ordinary had happened. There was no police cordon sealing off a crime scene, or stony faced constable standing outside the house as they did on TV. He noticed the curtains had been closed, but only because he couldn't see into the front room. Someone had definitely been inside after he left, but whether that was a good thing or not remained to be seen.

Gerard would've missed the notice, if its drawing pin had not remained firmly pressed into the door's centre, and attached to it was a torn corner of white paper and clear plastic. The rest of the page, and its protective covering lay discarded just off the doorstep. It was a generic police crime notification, which provided little in the way of information. There was a pre-printed contact number for the local station, and an unintelligible name and comment scrawled along the bottom. He tapped the number into his mobile, and pinned the torn paper back into place. The door wobbled slightly as he pressed the pin back in, and it was only then he noticed the frame was splintered in and around the main lock and hinges. The door looked like it had been forced, and he tried the handle which made the door wobble again but it didn't open. Still, a decent kick or well-placed shoulder felt as though it would easily finish the job off.

Rather than forcing the front door, Gerard thought to try the back of the house first. He cycled to the middle of the row of houses, where a gated but open entryway gave access to the rear of the buildings. Now wheeling the bike, he walked the lane until reaching the head high slatted wooden fence and gate at the back of Mandy's parent's house. The gate was bolted but had no lock, and he put his hand through the hole drawing the bar back. Gerard opened the gate as quietly as he could, and looked around to make sure no one was waiting to leap on him as he came through. The garden was empty, so he pulled in the bike and closed the gate behind him. Keeping his eyes firmly on the house, Gerard quickly walked through the garden but hesitated at the closed back door. The notice out front advised the police had attended, but he had no idea what was going to greet him inside. He half hoped the door would be locked and he wouldn't be able to get in, but the handle pulled down and lock clicked back when he tried. Gerard pushed the door wide open, but rather than walk straight in he stood his ground. He listened for any sounds coming from inside, but there was only the silence of an empty house. Instinctively his eyes sought out where Jeff lay not twenty-four hours before, but the body was gone and only a smeared layer of dried blood outlined the spot. He checked the rest of the room, and for a moment didn't notice anything different other than its general disarray. Then he began to realise there were blank places where things would normally have been. He couldn't be sure about the kitchen, but looking around the living room there was no doubt. The large flat-screen television which stood in the corner of the room was missing, and so were their expensive up-lighting floor lamps. Not only were the takings from the coffee shop gone, but also the solid wooden table and chairs it had been counted on. As he looked through the rooms, Gerard found it was the same all over. He went upstairs, and outside the bedrooms clothes had been stacked at the doors ready to be taken away. A couple of the stacks were knocked over, covering the upstairs landing. The scene reeked of someone being disturbed before they had time to finish removing what they'd came for.

Gerard neither needed nor wanted to be in the house any longer. He'd come back to see what happened to Jeff and Ellen, and possibly sequester their car. The police notice answered his first question, and with the amount of missing things he could hazard a guess as to the fate of the car. At least the Jeff and Ellen situation had been taken out of his hands, but he was back at the beginning again for transport. There was no one he could borrow a car from, and he'd no idea how to steal one. Unless things took an unexpected turn for the better, he would have to stick with the bike for his journey after all. It wasn't a thought he relished in his current condition, especially if he needed to opt for the longer solution at Stranraer.

As Gerard left the house he bolstered the front door as best he could from inside, shutting it tight against the damaged frame. He jammed the back of a kitchen stool under the door handle to give the lock some extra support, and then left the house through the back door again. His empty stomach was beginning to complain louder than the pounding head, with a lack of food making him feel even worse than he probably would have done with just his injuries alone. Gerard passed the garden shed, this time taking more note of his surroundings as his concentration wasn't wholly directed at the house. As with their home, the shed had been broken into, and its contents dragged out into the garden in search for something easily saleable. Mandy's parents went camping frequently, and their large tent, foldaway chairs, and other bagged parts lay strewn about. Camping was an activity Gerard never had much time for, but if the electricity was still off in his flat then their gas stove could be a godsend. Rummaging through the bags and boxes, he was able to recover a small single ring stove with a mostly full gas cylinder, and a tiny pack-away two-man tent which had seen better days. He stuffed the things into his now bulging backpack, and was about to stand up as something cold pressed against his temple. A growling, threat filled male voice spoke up beside him.

"Don't move you thieving little bastard, or I'll shoot you right on the spot."

6 BOBBY'S HOUSE

Gerard didn't move a muscle - as ordered. He had as much right to be there as anyone, but even with a half functioning brain he knew a gun against the temple would trump any counter argument he could think of.

"I told you scavenging bastards last night." A creaky, hoarse note sounded in the heavily Manchester accented tones, as the pressure on his temple increased. "You come round here thieving, and I'll make sure you bloody answer for it."

"I don't know what you're talking about." Gerard stutteringly replied, trying and failing to keep his voice steady. "I'm Mandy's boyfriend…I know Jeff and Ellen!"

The pressure from the gun barrel decreased almost immediately, and after a second or two disappeared altogether. Gerard chanced a quick look to the side, trying to figure out where his assailant stood, and was greeted with a pair of worn tartan-check bedroom slippers and beige flannel trousers shuffling away from him.

"Alright stand up slowly lad, and don't be stupid." The voice returned, this time with a little less aggression in its tone.

Again Gerard did as instructed, and turned slowly to look at the man as he stood up. The threatening voice in no way matched the profile of the person before him. The voice denoted strength and control, whereas this white-haired old man seemed almost unsteady on his feet. Any apparent frailty of the body had not reached his mind yet, as piercing blue eyes held Gerard with a stare that looked straight into him. The man's clothes and hunched-over appearance were the epitome of pensioner catalogue chic, while the solid looking revolver he held looked even older than its owners probable seventy plus years. But no matter the weapon's age, its damage end was still pointed at Gerard, and there wasn't a tremble in its direction towards him.

After a moment or two of further awkwardness, the gun-toting pensioner seemed to grudgingly accept Gerard may have some right to be there, and slowly lowered his aim towards the ground.

"Sorry about the misunderstanding son. I thought you were one of that lot back - no offence mind." He quickly added, thumbing vaguely over his shoulder as though Gerard would know exactly who "that lot" were. "She's not even loaded to be honest, more prevention than protection. It looks the part enough."

Gerard still didn't respond, not knowing how to, so the man pocketed the gun inside his jacket. He slowly backed out of the shed, dropping his voice as he did so, now thumbing back toward the house.

"Is the young girl with you? You do know about Jeff and Ellen?"
Gerard was about to say he was more than aware of Jeff and Ellen's situation, but didn't intend opening up to anyone who moments before was poking a gun in his face. Still, outright dismissal might not be the smartest move either, as he did seem to know something about last night, and if he could help fill in Gerard's blank spots then a conversation was well worth having. He decided to go along with it and see how things played out, even if the issue of the revolver put his new acquaintance in the highest 'handle with care' bracket.

"The same thing happened to Mandy as Ellen." Gerard said flatly.

"Jesus, I didn't know that. Decent people getting caught up in this mess all over."

The old guy shook his head, as he gave Gerard a good look up and down. "You feeling alright yourself? You're looking a bit white, and judging by those cuts and bruises you've been through the mill recently?"

"Yeah, you could say that." Gerard replied, bending back down to pick up his pack, and stumbling as he did so.

"Easy there friend." The man said, catching Gerard`s stumble with a surprisingly firm grip on his shoulder. "I think you might need to sit down before you fall down. I'm only next door if you need, and I don't want to be out here talking, not with all the craziness around."

Gerard was in two minds to follow. He'd no lack of things to do before leaving for Ireland, but definitely needed a break. His headache was beginning to be a constant knife-edge in the brain again, and a nauseating sickness swept over him if he moved too quickly. He accepted the offer of temporary sanctuary, and on his next attempt managed to pick up the backpack without toppling. He followed his new friend in silence out the gate at the bottom of the garden, and then back in through an adjoining one into next door.

"The name's Bobby by the way." Bobby said as they walked up through his well-tended garden, its flowerbeds and potted plants in full summer bloom.

"Gerard." He replied, shaking hands, and then let Bobby lead the way again toward his house.

"Nice garden." Gerard said, trying to fill in the silence with small talk. "Must take a bit of keeping?"

Bobby didn't respond, but instead opened his backdoor and walked into the kitchen. Gerard thought his comments had either been ignored or not heard, but once they were inside Bobby stopped and turned. Gerard could see moisture in his eyes, which he'd already tried to wipe away.

"That's my Dawn for you, loves the garden." Bobby started, looking passed Gerard to the outside again. Suddenly he seemed deflated, his voice a shallow echo in comparison to how it was when they first met. "At least it was until this bloody thing – Dawn, Ellen, and now Mandy. God knows how bad it's going to get if this is only the second day."

Bobby walked a few more steps into the kitchen. Gerard thought he was going to the living room, but he unexpectedly stopped and turned again, resuming his story with an anger filled tremor in his voice.

"She'd still be alright if those bloody hooligans hadn't been fighting outside last night. We wouldn't have even got involved if it wasn't next door. Straight away I rang the police and an ambulance, as it looked like things were getting ugly - even for around here. Then Dawn saw Ellen was hurt and out of it. Of course she had to go out and try to help. Ellen looked awful, covered in cuts and glass, blood all over her. God, at first we thought she must be dead there was so much blood, but she was still breathing. She came around pretty quickly, but straight off goes mental and scratches Dawn all up her arms and face. It was lucky for us the ambulance turned up when it did, though they put the fear of god in us with them all masked up and suited like there'd been a nuclear meltdown or something. We were told to go home, and did of course. Those boys had enough to deal without us getting in the way. They literally throw Ellen into one of the 'Paddy Wagons', and then the ambulance people go next door. It wasn't long after they brought out a covered stretcher from the house - Jeff, the poor bugger I soon found out.

But that was only the start of it. The ambulance leaves, and pretty much straight away Dawn gets ill. I ring for them to come back, while she goes up to bed to lie down. I wasn't gone ten minutes before there's smashing and crashing upstairs. I go up to see what's going on, and didn't even get in the bedroom door open before she attacks me."

Bobby held up his right arm, and for the first time Gerard noticed the bloodstained, poorly wrapped bandage on his forearm.

"I didn't know Dawn had that kind of strength left in her, especially to be wrestling and fighting me the way she did. In the end I had to keep her locked in the bedroom until the ambulance came back. All the while I'm pleading with her to stop as she was going to hurt herself, but I wasn't talking to Dawn anymore. It was something else trapped in that room, not my wife."

Gerard thought Bobby was finished, but he was only trying to compose himself after revisiting his own personal nightmare. With a sigh he continued.

"When the medics came back, they said people were being taken to the hospital wing at Strangeways' due to the number of cases, but I couldn't go with them as the prison wasn't equipped for it. Chances are they probably took Ellen and maybe Mandy there to. One of the ambulance crew bandaged my arm up a bit, but they'd no time for anything else. I was told to stay here, but knew it was just the fob off. Still, what choice did I have but wait and worry, and then after a bit I hear more commotion next door. Next thing those scumbags are carting out Jeff and Ellen's belongings like it was a house clearance. One of them even manages to find their car keys, and off it disappears in a cloud of rubber and smoke. Well I couldn`t take anymore after seeing that, and went a bit further than I should have - you know, with the stress and everything. I went out with the revolver, just for a bit of front as they wouldn't have listened to me otherwise, but it goes off - accidentally like. I tell you, it scared me more than them, but the place cleared out quickly enough. A few of the older ones tried it on to see if I was serious, but I couldn't turn back then and put a couple of rounds in the air to show them. Unfortunately that's why you were met with such a warm welcome. But its history now. Let me get you sat down, before you drop on the carpet."

Gerard followed Bobby from the kitchen to the front room.

"Make yourself comfortable somewhere, and I'll sort out a brew." Bobby left Gerard in the front room while he returned to the kitchen.

7 A SENSE OF DIRECTION

Instead of finding somewhere to sit, Gerard's attention was immediately taken up by the TV. The channel was on the BBC news, and unsurprisingly the topic was still IES.

"...spread of the virus has been tracked to a single point, originating in Manchester which fanned out through exits around the airport and central train station. A secondary inclusion zone has now been raised at Euston station in London, and reports of cases in other regions of the UK are being received. Public transport is suspended in affected areas, and flights from the airport in Manchester, and both flight and ferry crossings in Liverpool are currently cancelled.

The authorities are seeking this man..."

As Gerard watched, a different picture than the one he'd seen earlier appeared on the screen. This time the photograph was a grainy head and shoulders shot of a thin, middle-aged man with a greying goatee, and looked as though it had been taken for a passport or work identity card. The newsreader continued.

"...in connection with the outbreak – Dr. Nathan Harper, a lecturer at the university of Manchester and consultant for the St. Mary's genetic institute also in the city. Sources in Manchester have reported that an explosion in the university grounds earlier this morning occurred as checks were being carried out for evidence of unauthorized research. Bomb disposal experts are currently working in conjunction with the Health Protection Agency to ensure the University and surrounding area are safe from further devices.

The CCTV footage on screen shows Dr. Harper at the infection zones in both Manchester and London, but since leaving Euston station there have been no further confirmed sightings. Dr. Harper is considered highly dangerous, and members of the public are advised not to approach him, but to contact the police hotline by one of the following telephone numbers..."

The news report began to go over the previous details as Bobby returned with a tray of steaming tea, and set one of the cups on a small wooden ring-stained coffee table near to where Gerard stood. As he came into the room Bobby looked as though he was about to say something, but changed his mind when he refocused on the news.

"Bloody diabolical isn't it." Bobby said. "It's not like people have enough problems without others making up even worse things. I'd like to get my hands on that one at the minute. Bloody arthritis wouldn't stop me from throttling him I tell you."

With his blood up Bobby took a deep breath, and then with deliberate care slowly eased himself into an old armchair directly across from the TV. His seat of choice was older, and out of sync with the rest of the furniture in the room. At one point in its life, the over-stuffed chair had probably been an expensive purchase, but now it sighed as much as Bobby did while he settled into its battered dark-green leather.

"We should put that bugger in with those who`ve been got caught up in his thing." Bobby continued, trying to find his sweet spot. "I've been around the block enough, and this is well beyond me. You could bet your last pound we don't even know the half of what's going on. There's stuff all over the internet about that St. Mary's place even before any of this, though I bet those news people have been told not to say anything about it."

"The internet?" Gerard said quizzically. It was highly likely that any genetics lab would have a poor internet history, but Bobby the 'net-jockey' just didn't fit into Gerard's current opinion of the man.

"Aye, the internet. I'm retired not dead son. `Silver Surfer` package for those over sixty-five, or at least that's the box they want to tick at the minute. They can call me anything they want, as long as it`s discounted in some way. You'd be surprised what you can get up to on a pension, if you ask the right questions and plead poverty. But what difference does it make now eh?"

With that final last sentence Bobby internally struggled with his own problems again. Gerard could easily read him, though it wasn't difficult as they both had been through a similar experience. Bobby was trying to keep a brave face on things, but he was slowly faltering without his other half. Chances were he would give out completely at some point, and Gerard could only hope the pensioner wasn't waving the gun around again when it happened, or someone was definitely going to get hurt.

"Still, you've got troubles of your own lad eh?" Bobby spoke up, focusing his attention elsewhere so he didn't have to concentrate on his own problems for a minute. "What happened with the young girl?"

Gerard didn't particularly want to relive the previous day for a third time, but he told Bobby about his arrival at the flat, and the rest of the time just filled in behind it. Bobby listened, and let Gerard finish without interruption.

"Jesus, you had a night of it to." Bobby finally replied. "I was wondering where you'd picked those scrapes up from. It's a pity I didn't know who you were yesterday or I might've been able to have done something before all that. I don't know if you want my opinion, but I wouldn`t be too hasty trying to get back to Ireland if you have to make it on a pushbike. You could've used Jeff's car as you said, but you're a bit late now. Never had one myself. I hear what you're saying though, but it's a tough one to call. I'll be keeping these home fires burning no matter what, so if anyone knocks on next door I could let you know – only if you want mind."

Gerard thanked Bobby, and wrote his mobile number on a small square pad he was passed. Bobby stared at the number for moment as if trying to figure something out, and then bent over the far side of his chair muttering to himself as he did so.

"Ahh, here we are." He said after a minute, pulling out a battered looking Sunday supplement from a wobbling stack of papers, and handed the magazine to Gerard.

"This might come in handy. I know it's only a pull-out so there's no guarantee of accuracy, but it'll point you in the right direction."

Gerard took the magazine and flicked through the pages, quickly realizing this was a map of the country spread across a few dog-eared pages. He hadn't even begun to think about planning a cycle route, other than knowing the Motorway was a definite no-no on a bike. That would leave the minor roads, and an even longer journey with less regular signposting, so he could do with as much direction as possible. The scale of the map was large enough to show the motorways and main roads, even if there wasn't the greatest detail outside of that. The maps focus was more concerned on advertising space and which motorway service had a McDonald's restaurant, but it was a lot better than anything he had a minute ago. Gerard didn't want to seem ungracious, so he thanked Bobby again and put the magazine in his bag to look over later.

"Thinking on it though." Bobby continued pretty much straight away. "You'd probably be better with something printed off the net."

Bobby sat for a second, as though gearing himself up for the move, and then slowly rose from the seat with a well-rehearsed groan.

"Come on then, before I recline and it takes away my will to move altogether." Bobby shuffled his way to the door. "Anyway, I think I deserve a little relaxation after all this. I'll take you up to retirement central, and get us both sorted."

8 OLD DOGS AND NEW TRICKS

Bobby led the way up the thin staircase at a snail`s pace, and then along the landing towards a room at the rear of the house. He hesitated slightly as they passed the master bedroom. Gerard didn't said anything, as he didn't think upsetting their uneasy equilibrium would do either of them any good, but he couldn't help notice the damaged panels. The door was peppered with cracks and splinters, coming from inside the room where Bobby's wife had been trying to force her way out.

"Retirement central!" Bobby announced, opening a door at the end of the hall as if he'd just found the entrance to Nirvana. Both of them ignoring the elephant they'd just left in the hallway.

Gerard could hear the low electrical hum before he entered the room, and walking through the doorway he was met by a bank of three monitors placed on a makeshift shelf along the wall in front of him. The monitor to the left had the TV news on mute, the BBC again, with what looked like another regurgitated bulletin. The middle screen showed a black and white view of the front porch and path, leading up through Bobby's front garden. That screen flickered after a few seconds, and a new image came on. This time the view was from Bobby's back garden, but with the angle of the camera you could see a lot of next door - including the shed where they had their first encounter. The third larger monitor was off, but Bobby turned it on as he sat down at a battered looking swivel chair in the middle of the screens.

"Take a load off son." Bobby said, pointing to another chair in the left corner of the room under the window. Again it was a well-used seat, this time with a flower pattern that didn't match anything else he'd seen around the house, and was semi-hidden under piles of old magazines and newspapers. "Just dump that stuff on the floor." Bobby continued. "You'll need to excuse the lack of amenities. Other than Dawn coming in occasionally, you're the only person to have had the honour."

Once Gerard made space for the seat contents he sat down, and then tried to get a better view of the screens by pulling the chair away from a curtained partition that blocked off a large corner section of the room. A change in view of the middle monitor caught his eye, as the scene again moved from the roof to a wide shot of the street. A small speaker above the monitor began to emit a low pinging sound as a car passed by Bobby's house.

"I know, I know, the nosey neighbour from hell eh?" Bobby said laughing, seeing Gerard caught up in the screens. "True, I suppose." He continued. "Let's just say I like to know what's going on, even if I don't necessarily involve myself. Those pretend gangsters can knock the hell out of each other for all I care, and usually do every weekend, but for me it's just live reality TV - until last night anyway. Here's the workhorse." Bobby continued, changing the conversation as he patted one of the old PC's as if it was a favorite pet. "It's almost criminal what people virtually give away on that eBay and recycling boards. These computers were practically free as I picked them up, and all because they won't play the latest stupid games. Those security cameras, thirty quid for four sets through an auction. They have night vision, motion sensors - the works. A complete steal for a nosy old git like me, who likes to keep an eye on what's going on around him. Anyway, I'm letting my toys run away with me. I'll get you those directions printed, and then we can relax."

Bobby turned back to the screen, and began typing at the keyboard. After a minute or two of intense staring, and two strengthening glasses changes later, he found a site that would give him both a decent map and useful directions.

"Bingo!" Bobby said, finally bringing up the details. "You'll be alright with this one. I knew you could get directions for cars, but not bicycles. You learn something new every day eh? I'll start this printing. It was Stranraer, wasn't it?"

Gerard replied that it was, and watched as Bobby set the printer off.

"Right, that'll take a minute or two to print out. You don't mind if I have a smoke do you? Let me just slide passed you there."

Bobby wasn't waiting for a reply, and half pushed by Gerard to get access to the curtained off area of the room.

Gerard moved out of the way as best he could, and as the curtain drew back a strong amber light escaped which made spots jump in front of his eyes. As his sight adjusted he could see Bobby inspecting what looked like a small forest. The plants needed no introduction, as their unique aroma quickly began to saturate the room - Bobby's smoke of choice was Cannabis, and there was nothing amateur looking about the setup.

Bobby quickly returned from behind the curtain carrying a small tray and coloured glass jar. He fixed the curtain back in place, which Gerard noticed had a silver coloured thick rubber backing to keep the light and smell at bay. Bobby sat back down on his chair again, eyeing Gerard who was trying not to show his surprise at the drug-growing pensioner.

"Well that's as good a reaction as I could expect." Bobby said with a full grin, still looking at Gerard as he fought to keep his own face under control. "I doubted you'd have a problem with my little garden, but to be honest I'm beyond caring at the minute. Do you ever partake?..."

"Yeah, on and off. Mandy and me would occasionally, but it's my brother who could talk you to sleep about it. Seeing those in here was just a bit of a shock, well not a shock, but unexpected if you know what I mean." Gerard tried to sound relaxed about it, but he needn't have bothered as Bobby didn't look fussed either way.

"Yeah, getting on in years is a decent cover for most things. Not that I sell it or anything. Dawn has MS, and believe it or not it was the doctor who brought it up. I got the growing bug when I found the end product agreed with me to." He said with a chuckle. "The side effects from those prescription drugs were hard on Dawn, so anything was worth a go. I bought a few stupid little bags of low quality garbage to try and help her with the pain and appetite. But we couldn't afford to spend money on that every week. It did the trick for her though, so I looked into growing it myself. At least that way we didn't have to let everyone in on the secret, and knew we were getting the best of stuff. Thank God for YouTube eh?"

As Bobby filled Gerard in on his growing history, he worked the tray on his knees like a professional. With one last deft movement, he stuck the newly skinned joint into his mouth and lit it. The air quickly filled with a clinging sweet aroma, and placing the tray on the floor Bobby sunk back into his chair with a fuller relaxed sigh than he had managed downstairs. Seconds later an uncomfortable jabbing from his inside pocket prompted him to deal with the forgotten additional weight he was still carrying. Bobby reached into his inside jacket pocket, pulled out the gun and set it gently on the computer desk in front of him.

"Sorry again about earlier son." He said, looking at Gerard and nodding at the weapon on the table before lifting it again. Bobby opened the revolver and tilting back the gun he pushed the bullets out from their cylinders, three of which Gerard noticed were spent.

"I thought you said the gun wasn't loaded, those look an awful real to me." Gerard said with a half laugh, which was more nervous reaction than any response with humour behind it.

"Well, you looked like you were about to pee yourself when you saw it, so I had to say something." He chuckled. "And it's not like I was throwing my weight about or anything. I thought there was valid reason." As he spoke Bobby pulled a dark toned wooden box from a discreet slot beside the right hand monitor, and placed it on his lap. "One of the first things they tell you - never point a gun at anyone unless you're prepared to use it. That being the case, this box has been gathering dust for nearly as long as I've been around, and hasn't been opened in decades for anything other than the occasional cleaning. I wasn't even sure if it would fire to be honest, but some things are made to last."

Bobby opened the box, and inside Gerard saw the imprinted outline of the gun he'd been introduced to earlier. The molding was lined in a soft green cloth, with ammunition set into the case and cleaning brushes around the revolver. Bobby took the emptied gun, and absently rubbed over the dulled metal with a cloth, a distant look on his face.

"Smith & Wesson, Victory Model." He continued to clean the piece without looking up. "Belonged to my dad when he was in the home guard, near before my time. Of course you're supposed to return it when you're discharged, but I'd doubt that many did back then. Collector's item this, though now it might be evidence if last night was anything to go by. I got it after my old man passed, and probably would have handed it down to, but Dawn and me never had any kids."

Bobby checked the gun over again, peering down through the barrel as he did so to make sure it was clear, and then passed it to Gerard with the grip end first.

"You ever fire a gun, ever hold one?"

Although Gerard wouldn`t count himself in any way experienced, he wasn't a complete novice around guns. There'd always been a shotgun or the occasional rifle around the farm for hunting or vermin control, but he'd never used a pistol. Without being asked Bobby ran Gerard through the general points.

"It's simple really with a double action revolver like this. Both hands on the grip, face up, not sideways like you`re some sort of gangster.  Breathe in, hold it, then exhale slowly and squeeze the trigger when you`re ready. You have to put a bit of effort into firing it, but that's as basic as it comes."

Gerard turned the weapon over in his hands, aiming it like Bobby said and feeling the weight. This was a proper gun, a solid heavy piece of metal. The fact Bobby had an unregistered usable firearm still didn't sit well with him, but at least it had not been bought from the boot of some shady character's car. Normally Gerard wouldn't have went near it, but at the moment the oil smelling chunk was a weighty comfort in his hands.

With a little reluctance Gerard passed the gun back to Bobby, who with an unnecessary final polish put the revolver back in its box. In return Bobby passed Gerard the ashtray, with the still smoldering joint in it. For a second he was going to decline, but then took it anyway and inhaled deeply. Getting stoned might not have been the best idea with everything going on, and no doubt he needed to keep focused, but the last twenty-four hours had been so intense he needed some sort of release, if even just a little.

Creepingly the drug began to do its job, and for once Gerard's headache began to abate, not increase. Bobby finally had the printout ready, and in unison they swapped the joint back for the freshly printed instructions. The new map had much better detail than the one from the magazine, and generously Bobby had spread the print over a few pages. He`d also added directions specifically for bikes, so there were no life-threatening motorways to deal with. As Gerard studied the map, Bobby picked up a desk phone that rested on the same table as the monitors, and hit the button to redial his last number. He sat with the phone cradled to his ear for a minute, and then with a curse slammed the handset back into its holder.

"Buggering telephones. They give out a number but the bloody thing's either always engaged or just rings out. How are you supposed to know what's happening if you can't even speak to someone? The TV hasn't

mentioned the victims, or what's happening to them, and that number they're giving out is even worse than the one I'm trying. Even if you do get through to someone, they have no more idea than you."
Gerard nodded his head at Bobby's rant, agreeing wholly. Bobby was about to continue when his attention was caught by a scrolling update banner on the TV stating 'Army mobilised'. This was a new turn to events, and he turned the TV volume up to hear if anything useful was being said.

"...local emergency services are struggling to cope with the number of callouts, connected with what is now being classified as a serious countrywide health emergency. Government officials have advised that in the areas of highest impact such, as Greater Manchester and some parts of London, detachments from the regular and territorial armies are being deployed to bolster flagging services. A spokesman for..."

The report continued, but Bobby lowered the volume again with a sigh.

"That's it for us then kiddo." Bobby said, passing the joint back to Gerard after a final exhale of billowing blue and grey smoke. "If they're sending in the army then we're royally screwed. And if you want to get home then you'd better set off soon. First it will only be helping out, but the next thing there'll be a curfew, or more restrictions on travel. No matter what way they portray it, sending in the Army is never a good sign for anything."

"And what are you going to do? Are you still going to stay here?" Gerard asked.

"Don't you worry about me, someone has to hold the fort eh?" Bobby came straight back, lifting his arms palms up as though showing off his kingdom. "Anyway, I need to wait and see what happens to Dawn, and I`m too old to for all the messing about."

Gerard finished the joint, and stubbed it out in the ashtray. Even with his own problems, he couldn`t help but feel empathy for Bobby. At least Gerard knew there was healthy family waiting for him back in Ireland. At the moment Bobby could sink into oblivion, and no one would probably ever know. Gerard thought about getting up and making ready to leave, especially with that latest news, but he was too comfortable and sleepy. He loathed to move in case his pounding head came back to the foreground again.

"Tired son?" Bobby said, as he noticed Gerard struggling to keep awake.
"That'll be the Indicia mix in the smoke. For Donna's pain and my arthritis

mostly, but it'll definitely make you drowsy too. You'll be alright where you are for a bit, and you look like you could do with a kip."

Gerard barely heard his voice as the dark haze he waded through turned to sleep.

9 A BIT OF A SHOWDOWN

Ping…

Gerard knew he was still in Bobby's house. The same old furniture littered the place, though his carefully hidden forest grew out like vines from behind the sheeting. At the same time there was no mistaking this was a prison. He was in the back bedroom, but its windows had rusted bars and cracked glass in them. On the monitors he could see long metallic landings covered in pealing flower-pattern wallpaper, and security posts made of boards hastily stripped from lengths of uprooted flooring. Everywhere the cameras looked it was empty and silent, but instinct told him somewhere out of view the hordes were gathering en mass. They were waiting, and it was only a matter of time before the hunt began.

Beside him like she'd always been at his shoulder, stood Sigourney Weaver but as Ripley from the film 'Alien'. She had a motion-sensing tracker in her hand, which emitted a high-pitched ping at a steady interval. Neither spoke but communication wasn't necessary. They were in sync, and both knew the HarpIES were coming, ever closer and stalking.

Ping...Ping.

Ripley was shouting at him, from outside the open cell. Her mouth made words, but no sound came out. Still, Gerard knew what she was saying. They had to go, now, before it was too late - though deep down in his stomach he knew it was well beyond the time for leaving.

Ping…Ping…Ping.

Somehow Gerard was now running the length of the upstairs landing. He could see an open door at its end, and the feeling of safety emanating from the space was an almost tangible thing. But there were others, new people joining the race towards safety. Side doors opened, letting souls loose to barge and deny him safe passage.

"Run for the door, don't look back." Ripley screamed at him.

Ping, ping, ping...

Of course the HarpIES are upon them as they reach the door, which slams shut just out of reach. The runners collide into it, and each other, hammering and clawing, splintering the panels. Gerard felt hot, dead breath on his neck. Ripley is beside him again, but now she was also Mandy. He can't force himself to look at her. He can't bear to see the disappointment he knows is on her face. Shame flows through him, and though nothing is said he can feel her scorn upon him like bindings, a steeled grip. Then suddenly it's darkness which surrounds him again, and a shout from Mandy. But even this is something more felt than heard.

"Wake up!"

Gerard woke with a start. He remembered being chased, the fear and blind panic still trembling in his heart. He was awake now, and knew it was so. Still, he couldn't understand why the pinging of Ripley's scanner hadn't stopped?

The room was dark. Bobby had closed the bedroom curtains while Gerard slept, but their edges still let through a weak aura of light so he could tell it wasn't night yet. The security camera monitor faintly lit the room with an eerie monochrome glow, and the pinging came from the same source. He could see a group of people standing in the road, a short distance from the bottom of Bobby's front garden. They were arguing between themselves, and gesturing at the house. There was no volume on the monitor, but they were a short enough distance away and loud enough so that Gerard could still hear the conversation through the partially open window.

"I'm going over." An angry male voice spoke up. "I don't give a fuck. Denise and San are sick because of them, and if you aren't doing anything then I will. Either that crazy bitch or the old fucker with the gun is to blame, and I'll show them both."

"Have you not seen the TV? That shit's happening all over the place mate, and they`re right in it to..."

Although he'd only heard the end of the conversation Gerard knew reason was not going to have the upper hand with those who gathered outside. He stood in the middle of the room, indecisive about either trying to find Bobby or continuing to eavesdrop. His head had already begun to pound again, but there was no going back to the comfort of sleep.

Quietly opening the door to the landing, Gerard looked out. There was no Bobby, so he stealthily walked the hall to the top of the stairs and stopped again to listen. Still nothing notable above the rantings outside, no indication Bobby was about, and he couldn't call out for fear of being overheard. If Bobby was listening to the conversation, Gerard hoped he'd keep calm enough to not aggravate the situation unnecessarily. With any luck Bobby would be playing the 'wait and see' game before making a move which he might not be able to easily back down from.

Gerard slowly walked down the stairs, still trying to be as quiet and inconspicuous as possible. He got about half way down, and from his vantage was able to partially see into the front room. At first he thought his eyes were playing tricks on him, but a darker shadow quietly moved within the slightly lighter gloom. It was Bobby. He came to the door of the room silently, and beckoned for Gerard to come down.

Gerard joined him in the front living room, still keeping away from the doors and windows in case he was somehow spotted outside. Bobby had positioned himself at the back of the room. He was far away from the window so as not to be seen without someone peering directly through, but he could still look out and clearly hear the increasingly loud argument.

"These are the same jokers from last night." Bobby said quietly when Gerard reached him. "I recognise the loud one with the scratches on his face, and you might to. I'll not start anything, but I'm sure as hell not backing down from them."

"This is crazy." Gerard said. "What about the police?"

"I've already rang them." Bobby replied, his attention not faltering. "But I don't expect anyone to turn up, at least not until something happens. That's usually the case around here, and now it'll be worse."

Gerard could see Bobby was restraining himself, just itching for a reason to go out. This conclusion was compounded by the fact his gun was back out of its box again, and looked ready for use. Bobby seemed charged, almost excited as he fondled the grip of the pistol.

"Here we go." He said suddenly. The group had begun to move again, and Bobby left his hidden vantage to go to the front door and meet them head-on. "You stay back son, just in case. This isn't a fight you need to get involved in."

Even though Gerard didn't know what "just in case" might entail, he did not intend to hang back. Bobby's demeanour and posturing left little doubt he'd settled any lingering concerns relating to use of the gun, and with those outside already baying for blood then a clash was inevitable. If even to keep his own conscience clear, Gerard couldn't stand idly by while the old man went on a killing spree, or more predictably got himself killed. Gerard left the front room in Bobby's wake, and was in the hallway just as the banging started. He half expected to see Bobby limbering up for some kind of last stand, but he was motionless a few steps away - the banging wasn't coming from his door.

"Stupid buggers." Bobby growled. "Most of these idiots have lived here for years, and still haven't a clue who lives beside them."

Bobby took a deep breath, then opened the door and stepped out onto his porch with Gerard only a step behind. The group were within touching distance, and had surrounded Jeff and Ellen's front door expectantly while the scarred instigator shouted, huffed and puffed for someone to come out and face him. Just as the mob began to realise there might not be anyone in the house a set of spinning red and blue lights appeared at the top of the street, and a shrill siren cut through the dusk in intermittent bursts.

Immediately silence fell as a police car slowly rolled towards them. Initially it seemed only to be a single car, but as the vehicle got closer you could begin to make out the outline of a dark canvas topped lorry following close behind it.

"What the fuck is this?" The man who'd been banging on Mandy's parents door now focused on the new arrivals, his previous target all but forgotten as that age old adversary of the Police had arrived.

Gerard thought he could see darkened figures jumping down from the rear of the truck, and then felt a hand on his shoulder. It was Bobby.

"If you're going, now's the time son. Once this lot get it together, I doubt anything will be moving in or out." He said, pointing to the small convoy.

Gerard knew Bobby was right. The Calvary couldn't have turned up at a more opportune moment, but he had to take advantage of their misdirection. The officers from the squad car were immediately surrounded as they left the security of their vehicle, and while all eyes were directed at them Gerard followed Bobby back indoors.

"You grab your bag and get gone, if you're sure you still want to… " Bobby said. His question trailing off to see if Gerard's mind had in any way changed. But he knew it wasn't to be, so after a brief pause he continued as if the question hadn't been asked. "I think I've left everything of yours at the back door. I'll just check what that lot are up to, and be back to see you out."

Gerard went to the kitchen to collect his gear. He took a quick stock to ensure the latest additions were still there - tent, gas, and burner, then hooked the bag over his shoulder and went back towards the front door to see what was happening. Bobby met him as he reached the entrance to the living room, in his hands was the closed gun case.

"This wasn't how I'd ever envisioned passing it on, but those scumbags are already telling the Police about this. They might not believe them, or do anything about it, but I'm not taking any chances. Better you take it and not need it, than it end up in a furnace somewhere and be no use to anyone."

Gerard didn't take the box straight away. He was in two minds if the weapon would be more of a hindrance than a help. There was no denying a gun could be of great benefit, but at a minimum it would leave him with an illegal weapon to dispose of.

"You sure about this?" Gerard asked, reaching for the box but still not taking it.

"It's either us or them kiddo." Bobby said, pushing the box firmly into his hands. "I'd rather it be put to some good than melted for scrap."

Bobby let go of the box and then pulled a piece of paper from his pocket, holding it up for Gerard to see.

"I don't use it much, but I've turned my mobile on. I've written the house phone number on there as well, just in case you can't get through on the other. Ring or text me if you get stuck."

Gerard took the paper, and stuffed it into his jeans pocket. He thanked Bobby again, while being ushered out through the kitchen. At the door leading to the back garden Bobby unexpectedly grabbed him in a tight bear hug, and then literally pushed him out the door.

"Look after yourself son, and ring that number if you need it." Bobby shooed him away. "Use the path you came in on, and you won't have any problem getting out. Better be quick about it though."

With a final wave Gerard quickly walked away from the house, and out into the gathering dusk. It'd only been a few hours since he and his host met, and the majority of that time Gerard had spent sleeping. Still he felt a bond had formed between them, if only over their similar situations, and Gerard hoped he'd meet the old man again under better circumstances.

Leaving thoughts of better times behind, he turned his attention back to current events. Collecting the bike, Gerard forced the gun box into his pack so it closed, and slung the bag back over his shoulder. He was glad night was setting in as not only would it cover his leaving, but the pain in his head and eyes became more tolerable as the light decreased. Gerard left through the back gate, and stopped to hear what was going on around him as it closed. There was shouting and arguing at the front of the houses, and it sounded as though the police were still continuing to work on crowd control. The army would have a different and less subtle mandate, so there was no time to mess about.

No matter the urgency Gerard still walked the path with care, and stopped every few feet to listen again. The path was unlit and in the shade of the houses, making his way ahead almost pitch black. He'd nearly reached the corner where the path split and went left into the street he arrived on, or right and into another street when he heard a shuffling noise ahead. He stopped dead, but couldn't hear anything above the noise of the residents. Gerard was about to step out when he noticed a darker shadow clinging to the wall. The darkness moved slightly, and he froze again. He knew it was another person watching the street, someone who hadn't noticed his own quiet approach. There was no way to gauge their size or sex with the shadows and their crouched frame, but he couldn't take any chances. He began to back up, lifting the rear wheel of the bicycle so it didn't click as he reversed. Still looking ahead he saw another shadow crossing the mouth of path towards the main street, and then another. Gerard hesitated, debating if he should shout to those on the street or run back to the relative safety of Bobby's house. He continued to backtrack in the direction he'd come, but within moments the shouting at the front intensified and then there were gunshots.

Gerard didn't wait. He turned the bike around and jumped on, cycling as fast as he could and prayed for an exit to the path at the opposite end of the street.

10 HOME ALONE

Luckily for Gerard there was a top exit that also lead from the rear of the houses, and he cycled back to the flat without stopping. Along the roads there were other groups of people gathered around flashing lights in similar looking situations as there had been at Bobby's, and every turn brought new alarms or sirens to leap out at him. He kept his forward blinkers on, focusing only on returning to the flat before night fully set in. Nothing bar someone physically ripping him from the bike would have distracted from his goal, and he purposely ignored any random shouts or cries.

Gerard quickly locked the bike in its storage bunker again, and walked around to the main entrance. The building was normally noisy at this time, but today it was quiet and visibly absent of people. The sounds of everyday living were subdued, though probably due more to the lack of electricity than anything else. The only real signs of life came from the windows where flickering lights of the occasional candle glinted in the gathering dark. The power still wasn't back on so Gerard had to negotiate the emergency stairs once more. This was another shadowy, echoing journey, and he silently swore while peeking his way around corners lit only with his nearly dead bike light. Every echoing sound made him freeze in his tracks, and he constantly expected trouble at every turn. He breathed a sigh of relief when finally reaching his floor, but the feeling was immediately quenched as the flat door locked behind him again.

The oppressive silence and memories which flooded over him on the other side of the door tried their best to overwhelm. If there wasn't a need to get some things together, he would have turned around and walked back out again. But there had been enough delay already, and he now had a semi-visualised plan to stick to. Gerard went straight to work and trawled the flat for anything he could use, all the while trying not to think of Mandy when he had to move her personal things around. After half an hour he had tired of the ghostly search under faltering lights, and chose instead to berate himself about his limited electricity supply. There had been such a rush to leave Bobby's, he'd not thought much about the electric back at the flat for anything other than food. It hadn't occurred to him before now, but all his links to the outside world depended on electricity. With their usual power sources removed, any technology was only as good as its remaining charge. His mobile was already down to a couple of bars, and the laptop battery hadn't worked without being plugged into the mains since it was virtually new. He'd managed to scavenge a few candles in his search, which mainly consisted of the small scented bathroom variety and were feeble at producing light, but anything was better than the burglar's glow he stood in. He'd also found some batteries that could be used in his bike light, but how long they'd last was another question. Of the six batteries only two were new, with the remaining being recovered from the TV remote control and the bedroom alarm clock. All in all if the electricity situation wasn't resolved soon, he'd be blind, deaf and dumb to any outside news by the morning.

Gerard opened the double doors that led to a small step-on balcony. The flat was stuffy after being closed all day, and the smoke from the candles was already beginning to get into his eyes. He stood looking out from the vantage point, trying to see how much of the area was still without power. Barring a few spots where the larger businesses had their own emergency generators, the immediate vicinity was mostly in darkness. Further off the lights of the city winked on as they always did, and the empty dark space before him made him think about being back on the island again when he would stare out over the sea to the distant lights of mainland Ireland. The thought gave him no comfort, but rather enhanced his feelings of isolation. He took in the scene until a growling from his stomach reminded him again that he still hadn't eaten properly since yesterday, and left the patio doors open to return inside and finally prepare something to eat.

Renewing his search Gerard went through the kitchen cupboards for anything that could be easily cooked on the single burner camping stove. Tinned soup was the most convenient and simple fare he could muster, and after an age of slow rolling bubbles the chicken smell had generated some appetite in him. He finished the food quickly, and now he`d started hunger took him over. Even though the fridge had no power all day its contents were still edible, if a little warm, and he greedily ate the safest things rather than see them wasted.

The rag-tag meal made him feel a little better, and with a full stomach Gerard sat down on the sofa with night deepening around him. It was too late to leave now, and stupid to contemplate doing so since his cycle would then be through the night. Staying longer in the flat wasn't ideal, but it was the safest place to wait until it began to get light again. The cycle to Scotland would take all his energy, so he needed to conserve what he little had and rest. That being said, there was no way he could face the bedroom. Being surrounded by Mandy's personal things was nearly too much already. The sofa would have to be his makeshift bed for the night, if any sleep was on the cards at all.

Even though Gerard was locked away, a cloud of apprehension still slipped over him. Maybe it was the unnatural quiet of the residence, but every noise, whether he thought it was from inside the building or out in the dark streets had him on edge. He tried not to think about what lurked out of sight, and instead looked over the maps and directions Bobby provided, until the phone vibrated in his pocket and gave its text message received tone.

'Tried to ring, can't get through. Where's my call? Have you left yet? Call me, text, anything!!!'

The text was from Motty. With everything that happened Gerard`s earlier commitment to ring him back had been completely forgotten.  He checked the signal on his phone.  The display showed only one bar, then turned to `No Service`, and a second or two later flicked back to the single bar again. Normally there would be a full signal in the flat, but he had to assume the earlier explosion was messing with the local phone towers.

With the signal problems and his mobile only having a quarter of its battery remaining, Gerard didn't ring Motty back. Instead he wrote a quick message, saying he would call tomorrow when he managed to re-charge the phone. He sent Bobby a message at the same time, as he wanted to know how things ended when he left. After sending both texts Gerard went to the open balcony doors to see if he could get a better signal. The phone just flashed 'Sending...' on and off, so he left it there hoping there would eventually be enough reception to allow the messages through. This would use a minimum of power compared to calling, and once gone he could turn off the phone and save its remaining battery.

Staying by the open balcony of his dark island, Gerard closed his eyes and listened to the sounds filtering up to him. On balmy nights in better times, Mandy and he had sat in the same place listening to the rhythms of the city, with a few beers and a spliff or two to elevate the mood. The beat of the cities heart would rise up to them - music, the chatter of people, laughing and traffic, the lifeblood of the city. Tonight there was a very different feel, and though a lot of it could be put down to his own paranoia and fear, there was no doubt this was a very different animal he listened to.

Staring down into the grey-blue gloom of the street, Gerard looked and listened for signs of life. Every now and again there was the distant sound of glass breaking, a shout in the darkness or running echoing footfalls. Sirens and lights from emergency services flashed in adjoining darkened streets, all of which helped to draw a bleak mental picture of the situation at ground level.

A scream rang out from somewhere just below him. It was a sharp cry, cut off suddenly at mid-point, and then nothing after but an ominous silence. He didn't know where the sound came from, and waited for something else to happen, but nothing was forthcoming. No matter where it originated, he wasn't going to take any chances. Going back inside Gerard took a stool from the small kitchenette, and propped the backrest under the front door handle to help jam the lock in place. Then he returned to the kitchenette and rummaged through the drawers looking for the most solid knife, and placed this on the coffee table in the main room. Between the gun, knife and rolling pin he was gathering a bit of an arsenal. Gerard opened the gun box and stared at the revolver inside, wondering if he could pull the trigger on another person - even if they were infected, or if it was to save his own life. He couldn't say his brief training at Bobby's made him feel any better about it, but the gun was a comforting last resort no matter what.

He was now in even less of a mind to sleep, so Gerard pulled a chair up to the open balcony and sat down again to watch the streets through the slatted railings. At first he thought the shadowy movements were only his imagination, but after a while he knew it couldn't all be so. It was difficult to tell the real and imagined apart from his position and distance, but soon some of the shadows began to emit small lights. Shortly after the same lights started appearing inside the businesses of the buildings across from him, the thin shafts of their torches cutting through the dark.

"Good old Manchester scallys." Gerard muttered quietly to himself. No matter what the problems around them, the robbers and looters were always ready to take advantage. He laughed at the thought, then remembered Mandy's parents and it wasn't so funny anymore. They had lived in the same housing-estate house most of their adult lives, and the ambulance had barely left their street before the casual stripping away of their possessions started. Jeff and Ellen had been lucky to have a neighbour like Bobby, but there were not too many left like him. He was as 'old school' as you could get, a soul with decency, and someone who kept an interest in those around him even if it had started to get a little Orwellian. Knowing your neighbours and neighbourhood didn't follow with today's style of living. It was a problem Gerard himself added to, as he couldn't have told you a name or anything else about those who lived around him in the flats.

A shout from the street directly in front ripped him from his thoughts, and Gerard stood up to look over the railings for a better view. A torch had fallen on the road, and in its rolling beam two figures were caught struggling on the ground.

"Get the fuck off me you crazy bitch." A male voice was shouting, his voice rising in pitch as the struggle continued. "I said...Fuckin' cunt, aahhhh."

Another figure raced out from the dark, shown only by the fleeting movement of shadows across the ground. At first Gerard thought someone was trying to help, but he heard another garbled scream and then only silence. Now it was as if the first attack started a chain reaction, and another scream rang out, this time definitely from somewhere inside the block of flats. Gerard returned from his position on the balcony to listen, but there were only muffled noises, nothing to give an indication as to what was happening or where. There was a loud bang, a sound he recognised as the heavy metal fire door hitting the corridor wall on his floor. With the weight of the door, the noise could only have been caused by someone coming through with force. They could have been there for any number of reasons, but Gerard didn't intend to be the hero and find out. Every horror film in history had its victims going out to check on weird sounds when the lights were out, and he wasn't falling for it. If something was going to happen then it was going to be on his terms, so instead of opening the door Gerard looked through the security viewer, but it was too dark to see anything. He backed away again from the door, only realising when he saw his own shadow in front of him that the changes would still be noticeable on the wall outside through the viewer's eye. It was too late though. Something heavy struck the door, and it shuddered in its frame again, twice in quick succession as a weight was again thrown against it. A loud cry issued from out in the corridor. The noise sounded animal, a sound of torment and frustration, then silence again which made what came before all the more unbearable. The time seemed to stretch endlessly even though it was only a few minutes, and eventually Gerard thought he could hear noise further down the corridor at the empty flat on the end. He took the chance and went to the coffee table, straight for the box with the pistol, pulling the gun out. Comforted by the heavy oil smelling metal, he sat down facing the front door and waited for the next move to be made. He was still waiting as the first dawn pre-light began seeping through the windows and he began to think about leaving again.

11 FIRST LIGHT

As the grey dawn filtered through, Gerard rose from the sofa to pack away the last of his things. Activity from both inside and outside the building had all but ceased hours earlier, the final movement of note being an ambulance with Police escort which had pulled up outside. Gerard would probably have missed them in his doze, but their lights blazed through the darkness. A screech of tires told this hadn't been their chosen destination, as they nearly ran over the person whose attack he'd witnessed earlier. But they did stop while the body was checked, and two men in plastic suits quickly lifted the remains and carried it to the rear of the ambulance. Gerard expected some reaction to their finding a corpse in the street. He thought that maybe they would search the area for more victims, or even HarpIES carriers. He thought they'd at least make enquiries in the local area, knock on some doors and wake the neighbours, but none of that happened and both vehicles sped off again as soon as their way was clear. At that point Gerard resumed his vigil, fitfully dozing on the sofa with its direct view to the front door.

Placing a rucksack on the coffee table, he got his belongings together. 'Travel light' were the watchwords, as everything would be carried, so only the bare minimum could get in. The rent on the flat was good for another few weeks, so there was no need to take everything he owned. If things got better he'd be back before those weeks were up. On the other hand if things continued on their downward spiral, then some CD's or an extra pair of jeans wouldn't count much towards his survival strategy anyway. The rucksack was still fit for bursting by the time Gerard forced the tent, stove, half a loaf of bread, his mobile charger, two tins of food, and a bottle of water into it. He took the remaining bullets from their box and put them in a zipper pouch on the back, and finished the kit-out by filling the other outside pockets with his remaining candles, batteries, a fork, route printout, and finally the kitchen knife whose long serrated blade stuck out prominently from the bottom of the pack.

Turning on his mobile again, Gerard hoped the signal would have sorted itself out, or there'd at least be some new messages to help him gauge the next move. Nothing came through while he watched the screen, but he left the phone on in the hope it would pick up a signal. He was as ready as possible, and lifted the bike light off the table to use on his way back down the stairs. In his other hand he carried the pistol. If the earlier street attack had shown him anything, it was that he needed to be able to stand on his own, and his best asset was the gun, like it or not. It was stupid to have the revolver with him and not prepare it for use as long as he was careful.

Looking through the spy hole again, there was still only a grey blur visible outside. He removed the chair from behind the door, and undid the lock as silently as he could. Gerard immediately steeled himself against possible attack, and opened the door with the safety chain still on to afford him a little time and protection if anything happened. He looked up and down the corridor as best he could, checking for movement and panicking at the new shadows the door created as it moved. He took his torch and shone the light up and down the corridor. It was clear. If he was to leave it was now or never, and never was not a suitable option.

Undoing the chain Gerard let himself out, securely locking the door behind him again. As it shut something made him look towards the darkest end of the corridor - a movement only noticed from the corner of his eye. Gerard swung around, pointing the gun and torch in the same direction, both of his hands shaking to the point where firing with any accuracy would be near impossible, but nothing was there. He followed the torch beam around the hallway, and re-checked the corners, re-checked everywhere. He was only freaking himself out. It was a false alarm.

"Jesus man, get a grip." Gerard said to himself, trying to get his heart rate and breathing back under control. "You've a gun for God's sake, buck up." And with a deep breath he walked to the emergency exit stairs, torch and gun still pointed shakily forward, even if now it was slightly less so.

The fire door to the staircase was partially open, and he pulled it wide, thoroughly checking every corner and the darkest spots to ensure they were clear before going through and fully closing the door behind him again. Years of film violence, cop shows and console gaming provided some knowledge of how to check his surroundings. He cast his light down the stairwell, but the limited power of the torch quickly lost intensity if shone too far, so he still stopped and listened every few steps in case the echoing sounds were being made by someone other than him. He walked down three levels without any problem, and then another. Reaching the first floor he could see something near the foot of the stairs at the next turning. He couldn't make out what it was, but it wasn't large enough to be a person. Still, that was no reason to be careless so soon, and he cautiously walked down another few steps for a better view. Staring intently, it took him a moment or two to register what he was looking at, and then it struck him. It was an arm, a severed arm!

Even though he was still at a distance, Gerard's natural instinct was to reel away from the partial limb. He missed his footing on the stair behind, tried to recover, but slipped and went down. He instinctively put his hands out for protection, letting go of the gun and torch in the process. Gerard tumbled downwards, his momentum carrying him to the bottom of the staircase where he somehow ended on his front facing back up the stairs again. He felt wet on his hands, and held them up in the flickering bicycle light. They were covered in a dark, almost black looking liquid that dripped from his fingers in thick globs. Panic welled up in him, passing unhindered through his shaken frame. This was blood, lots of blood. Gerard's initial reaction was that he must be injured, but then he remembered the arm. Realisation sank in, there was too much blood for it to be just an arm – this was a kill.

Gerard scrabbled for the gun, whose clattering descent had stopped a few steps above him. It was within reach, but he slipped in the blood, his fingers just connecting with the pistol to send it spinning further out of reach. A screech behind him confirmed his worst fears, the noise creating a frozen shard, which struck straight through his core. The Harpie was still there. He lunged for the gun again as a solid weight hit him heavily on the back, knocking his breath out. He tried to push up on all fours, feeling the sharpness of nails and teeth trying to rip into him from behind. The Harpie struggled to get to him, its attack hampered by the full pack on his back. Gerard tried again to get up, but now his arm slipped beneath him, flipping him over on his back. Immediately the Harpie went berserk, screaming and thrashing wildly behind him, pinned between Gerard and the stairs. Pressing his new advantage, Gerard tried to stay on top and began elbowing backwards with as much force as he could gather. Momentarily the struggling behind him became even more intense, the stairwell filling with anguish laden garbled screams. Gerard didn't stop until all movement ceased, then finally he released the clips on his pack and struggled back to his feet. Slipping over to where the gun lay, he grabbed the revolver and drew it level with the Harpie, ready to fire. He hesitated, there was no sound, movement, or forthcoming attack. Gerard grabbed his pack, but it snagged on something. He pulled the bag harder, and as it came away the stomach contents of the woman slopped out after. The kitchen knife, whose blade stuck out from the rucksack side pocket had embedded itself in the Harpie when he'd flipped over, and cut a large jagged wound in her while they'd struggled.

Turning from the gore and putrid smell Gerard vomited. He sat down with a bump, close to where the Harpie's body intermittently twitched, while the flow of blood and guts began to taper off. He could not help but look at the woman. She was no longer a threat, a Harpie, or an attacker, but a person again. This was a victim who he just killed, whether it was accidental, necessary or otherwise. Gerard thought he recognized her as one of his neighbours, but couldn't be sure and didn't want to be either. The literal blood on his hands would take more than water to wash away, and the last thing he wanted was to add a person to the body in front of him.

With his adrenalin fading, the back of Gerard's head and shoulders began to sting. His backpack had provided some protection, but on occasion the Harpie still found a way around it. He rose from the congealing bloody puddle, the metallic taste and smell intensifying as he moved. Gerard felt like being sick again, but forced it down. He'd been attacked, but it didn't change the plan. If anything it made getting out of there even more of a priority, but he couldn`t leave as he was and needed to get clean. He limped back up the stairs, and into the flat again. There was nothing for it but to strip off completely and throw the ruined clothes outside on the balcony. He washed himself and redressed, then removed his belongings from the soiled and torn bag. The rucksack was ruined, completely drenched in blood on the outside, but at least its waterproofing had protected the contents. He moved everything to another holdall, and then left the flat again. He couldn't look at the woman as he passed her on the stairs. The only thing he could force himself to do was cover her with a blanket, and then focus on the journey ahead.

12 CITY EXIT

Even with the eventful start, it was still early enough to leave the city and not have any significant impact on his time. Whether the residents of the other flats had left already or continued to hide in their apartments Gerard would never know, he was just thankful there was no one else to deal with as he collected his bike. He was finished with the place, and couldn`t wait to get away from the soured memories that now scarred it for him.

Looking over the M61 motorway from an overpass which ran above it, Gerard watched the traffic limp along. Until now he'd only followed the minor roads which ran virtually parallel with the motorway, but these were also getting jammed and his curiosity had prompted him into cycling the short distance to the main road for a look. He didn`t think he would be leaving the city alone, but the scene below could only be described as one of chaotic exodus.  He'd seen the beginnings of the tailback before even leaving Manchester, but that wasn`t unusual on any day. Still, the problems people currently faced were not only due to the volume of traffic, but also those leaving were trying to take everything they owned with them.

Gerard's perch on the bridge only provided a perspective until the road turned away, but even from here he could see roughly tied pieces of furniture and massive suitcases precariously stacked on vehicles that were definitely not up to the job of carrying them any distance. Before him there was a car whose load hadn't been secured correctly, and it was now parked on the hard shoulder as the occupants tried to recover their belongings that had spilt across the lanes. Other cars were in the `hard shoulder` graveyard to, but for seemingly different reasons. One vehicle had over heated, and sat with the bonnet open and steam flying out. Another looked to have run out of fuel, or could have broken down for a multitude of reasons that slow moving traffic brings out in those who are ill prepared. The motorway service vehicles were nowhere to be seen, if they were still responding to calls at all. This left the occupants with two choices: Stay indefinitely, but in hope that help would be along sometime. Alternatively, lock the car and leave everything at the side of the road to be gloated on and picked over like vultures by those still moving.

Gerard left his fellow escapees to their personal struggles, and rode back to the minor road he'd previously been following. Even in the short time it had taken him to get to the motorway and back, the amount of people using the secondary roads had increased sharply. He was still able to slide by the worst of it, being on two wheels. A fact he heard vocalised by more than a few of those going nowhere. As the next hour wore on, the travel situation grew worse. Overflow cars had started to break down on the minor roads, making it virtually impossible to go any further as they straddled the paths and verges he'd been using when the regular traffic stopped. Judging by the increasingly hungry eyes and comments of those he passed, Gerard's paranoia told him it was only a matter of time before someone tried to take the bike. Cycle or not, it was the only thing that moved, and he didn't feel up to a fight if it came to it. He'd only been travelling a couple of hours, but already felt exhausted. The attack in the flats had jarred his other injuries again, and any real effort or exertion sent sharp pains through his head. Gerard could barely see through the brightness of the summer day, squinting in the light that was already subdued behind his sunglasses. He made the decision to stop and rest for a couple of hours, just until the roads got quieter. He studied the map, but couldn't decide on the best place to go. In the end it was closeness of location that held final sway, and he decided to check out a small forest he'd just passed. A better spot to rest could have been found, but he only wanted to get out of the sun. There was a Motorway services within a short distance, but a location like that would come with its own set of human problems. Gerard settled for a quick hideaway rather than services, company, or those who would try to fleece a lone traveler, and took his bike down an ungated access road toward the trees.

The access road quickly turned to a dirt track, which dipped down and ended in a circular bare patch a short distance into the group of trees. Judging by the neat rows and similar average height of everything around him, he guessed the place was man-made. It wouldn't be classed as a forest, but more of a copse due to the small size. It was a lone island of trees. A last stand in a sea of farmland grasses and networking roads, but the place was faring poorly. Where Gerard stood the front lines of trees had already been cut back, and the exposed grey earth stood out like a scar across its face. The felling cuts were new, and you could still smell the sap and chippings in the air. Still, it didn't look as though anyone had been there for a few days so he should be safe enough to stay for a while.

Gerard thought things would be easier in the shade, but he felt little better. He was weak and aching, his head spinning like he was about to faint or pass out. Gerard dragged his bike and belongings a few feet behind the cut line, so they wouldn't be immediately visible if anyone came down the lane. After quashing nearly half his water he opened one of the food tins, and started the gas stove. Lying still in the cool, with his eyes and mind firmly closed to everything but breathing he began to feel more human again, and eventually pulled out the printout map and magazine Bobby had given him from his bag. The next stage of his journey was a relatively straight forward route up the **A**6, and then onto the A75. This would get him to the west coast of Scotland, and within reach of Dermott's boat. He hoped with the city behind him the traffic would start to thin out, especially as he made his way into the less populated areas of the country and kept to the lesser roads.

A low "beep-beep" from his pocket snapped Gerard's attention away from the route, and had him delve into his jacket. It was the mobile, but the noise wasn't a call or text. He knew the sound even before looking - it was a battery notification, and sure enough the indicator was blinking red on and off at the last bar. He had a signal now, a poor one, but there were still no messages. With a final dying shrill, the phone screen went blank and the mobile turned itself off completely. He stared at the useless device for a minute, deflated, cursing his stupidity as he'd forgot to check and turn it off earlier. Now he would have to make a detour to charge the phone, or find someone who would let him borrow theirs. He couldn't just go to a pay phone either, for even if he found one that worked, with no power to his own mobile he'd no idea what number to call Dermott on. He was going to have to make an unscheduled stop at the motorway services after all.

His phone issue wasn't helping to ease stress levels, so Gerard dropped the subject as there was nothing he could do about it for now. His thinking was still muddled, with the simplest task taking a lot more effort than usual. The tinned Bolognese he'd been heating was finally warm enough to be edible, and he forced the food down. By Gerard's watch it was getting to just before one o'clock in the afternoon, and in the hollow he could already tell it had passed noon due to the difference in the light. With no homes or streetlights lamps, and his camp in the shadow of the trees, it would get dark there as soon as the Sun dropped below the high false horizon. Luckily it was summer, and dusk wouldn't be until eight o'clock at least. He could afford to sleep for a few hours, and hopefully clear his mind and fatigue. This would also give the traffic a chance to reduce, let the heat of midday cool off, and he should still be able to reach Scotland before it was too dark.

Gerard forced himself to pack away his things again, so at least he`d be able to leave when he wanted. Again the meal helped him feel a little better, but then he stood up too quickly and the movement sent his head spinning. Instantly he felt the renewed energy leave him, and a smell of burning, tinged with something sour crept over his senses. He felt heavy, and in the same breath a thick weightlessness enveloped him as though he'd just jumped in the deep end of a pool.

"You need to sleep love." He heard Mandy say, and could feel her presence behind him.

"Yeah." Gerard replied, neither unsurprised nor anxious at her sudden appearance. It was as if she'd never been away. "I'm will...Sorry I left." He could smell her scent, and feel her breath on his neck. He wanted to face her, but knew that in turning the spell would break. He was still a coward, and only forgiveness would ever let him meet her eye again.

"I know baby, but there's no way back on that road. You need to think about yourself now. You need to look down."

Gerard did as she said. There was a figure on the ground before him, but it took a moment for recognition to set in at this normally unseen angle - he looked down on himself. It was an empty epiphany though, as if he was not only cut off from the physical self but his emotions as well, a voyeur presiding over a life he had little or no stake in.

"Is this it then?" Gerard said. The statement spoken in the same detached manner he felt.

"Up to you babe. Stay or go, but you've got to want it either way."

Gerard continued to look down on himself, his consciousness an alien entity to the body below. But at the back of his mind he could already feel a tugging, a drip of synapses re-firing, pinpricks of life flowing back into his bones like cool water in a parched throat.

"You've gotta' want it babe!" Gerard heard Mandy say again.

Her voice grew distant, as an empty blackness once more rushed up to consume him.

13 THE BRIGHT OF THE NIGHT

Gerard came around, the metallic taste of blood on his lips. He tried to gather himself, but his head was still swimming. The rough camp stood in shadowy darkness, which only further served to disorientate him. Gerard struggled to his feet, staggered a little, and then toppled backwards as his foot caught the stump of a tree. He fell flat on his back, and this time stayed where he was while trying to make out which way was up. His unconscious interlude felt like only moments before, but the sky told a different story and he stared up at a darkening deep blue of evening.

Beyond his secluded hollow a scream rang out. Now he sat bolt up, trying to listen past his pumping heart, straining to hear if anything else followed it. There was noise in the distance, but he couldn't tell if it was relevant to the general sounds of the motorway and breeze rustling trees, or if there was something more to be concerned about. Either way he wasn't doing himself any favours by staying in such a vulnerable position, so he slowly began to grope around for the bag where he'd placed the torch and gun earlier for safe keeping. Noticing a darker lump slightly away from him, Gerard reached out and was rewarded with his belongings. He hurriedly tried to find the right pockets in the dark, checking more by touch than anything visual.

"No, no, please, aaghh..." The cry was definitely close to him. He couldn't tell which direction it came from, but if he could make out words then it was close enough to be concerned.

He found the torch, but left it switched off. His eyes were slowly getting used to the dim, and he began to make out the objects around him. Gerard felt around his bag again and found the gun, nearly ripping the pocket in his haste to get the revolver out. Now he was armed Gerard listened again. There was still nothing out of the ordinary, and he tried not to let his imagination lead him to possible horrors that were not there. As the seconds dragged, he began to hope that whatever happened had passed him by, but before he could start to relax again a blinding white glare lit up the trees. Any night vision he'd gained was instantly destroyed by a set of headlights. The bright halogen bulbs immediately threw the area into sharp stark focus, as the vehicle uncomfortably bounced its way down the dry rutted dirt and came to a sliding stop in the open space in front of Gerard's makeshift camp. The front drivers' side of the vehicle faced him, and as the blinding main beam's focus was pointed away he could see the lights were from a 4x4. The car had two occupants, both of which were in their early twenties at most, and looked panicked. With their lack of deftness in driving, and care used as the car rode the track, the vehicle was almost certainly stolen. The windows were down, but even over the loudness of the bass pounding dance music he could hear arguing inside. Gerard could see the angry face of the passenger as he pointed and shouted at the driver.

"Just get her the fuck out of the car!"

"I'm not touching her, she's all fucked up. You fuckin' do it!" The driver shouted back at the passenger.

"Didn't stop you sticking your dick in her though did it! Dirty bastard." The passenger came straight back.

"I wasn't the only one, you did an..." He replied.

"And?" The passenger talked over the other, trying to assert his authority. "Dump her, or I'll take the car and throw you both out here. I'm not having that skanky cunt anywhere near me."

Angrily the driver got out of the car, and opened his rear side door. The passenger exited as well, and gloatingly followed to make sure his instructions were carried out.

"Hurry the fuck up, we`re supposed to have dropped this off already." The passenger barked as he idly watched.

With the rear door opened Gerard could see who the argument was about. A girl was slumped, almost flat on the large back seat, shaking. She looked as though she was having a fit, and for an instant Gerard flashed back to when he'd seen Mandy in a similar condition. The driver tentatively reached into the car, grabbed the girl by the shoulders and began to drag her out. The passenger looked on, standing back a little from the scene with a smirk on his face.

At the side of his vision Gerard saw something moving quickly through the shadows, caught in the glare of the headlights. He thought it was a trick of the light, but the shadow quickly became a running person. With a growling scream the new arrival slammed into the driver, knocking him into the car and then both of them fell to the ground. Everything happened so fast it took a second for Gerard to realise what was going on in the confusion. The driver was being attacked.

Without thinking Gerard got up and made towards the tangled pair. He still had the gun in his hand, and ran across the open space while aiming the pistol. The driver struggled, and Gerard tried to hold his aim steady, hoping for a clear shot in the confusion. He saw his chance, and squeezed the trigger like he'd been shown. Instead of the loud bang and recoil he'd expected nothing happened, not even a click. The gun wouldn`t fire. He tried to pull the trigger again, but there was still no result.

"Fuckin' Shit." Gerard thought he knew what had happened, there must be a safety catch Bobby hadn`t mentioned. It was a mistake he'd scoffed at in films where a rooky gun user fell into the same trap.

Fumbling with the weapon he tried to find the safety catch, but there was none. He brought the revolver back up, his finger still firmly pressuring the trigger, and this time the gun fired prematurely. The Harpie never flinched, as the shot barely grazed her and instead hit the driver. With full force Gerard now pulled the trigger again, then again, and this time had a more successful result. The head of the Harpie virtually exploded in front of him, disintegrating into chunks of flesh, bone and brain. Hastily Gerard pushed the almost decapitated Harpie aside, and bent down to check on the driver. He was still wary of the woman he had just dragged off, as there were too many horror films in his history where a 'final bite' scenario occurred after the threat was supposedly over. However, that wasn't going to happen here. It couldn`t. There was barely anything left for the Harpie to bite with, and the lifeless torso remained slumped over on the ground.

The driver looked beyond help to, at least as far as Gerard could tell. He would have enough difficulty locating his own pulse under optimal conditions, never mind finding it on someone he'd just shot in the dark. But even without that marker he knew things were not going to end well for the driver. There were deep arterial strikes from the Harpie, where the resulting blood loss and shock would still have left him in a critical condition no matter Gerard's actions.

The adrenalin quickly drained from Gerard, and as it did nausea rose up to meet the fading endorphins. He began to shake, and tried to get up but the bile erupted too quickly in him. All he could manage was to turn away from the scene and vomit.

A door slammed shut next to him, and the engine of the 4x4 gunned into life again. The vehicle immediately roared off with high revs, kicking up earth and debris as its wheels tried to find purchase on the loose dry surface. There was no room to turn, so the driver tried to reverse back up the dirt track. Gerard stood in the glare of the bouncing headlights and shouted for him to stop, bringing his hands up in front in an effort to show he didn't mean any harm. There was a loud bang and recoil from his hand, then immediately the car jolted and revved wildly. Its reversing meandered journey was cut short as the vehicle swung violently to the left, and then crashed into a tree with the horn blaring. Gerard dropped the gun as if it had turned molten, and ran the short distance to the car praying he was wrong in what he thought had just happened. He'd pegged it correctly, but didn't want to believe what he`d just done. A few seconds ago the gun wouldn't work at all, and now he was directly responsible for the shooting of two people.

Gerard opened the drivers' door and looked into the car. There was blood and gristle on the headrest, dripping down in lumps, and the driver was slumped over the wheel.   He didn't want to reach in but the horn would attract attention, so he grabbed the driver by the shoulder and pulled him back to stop the noise. The shot had come in through the front windscreen, and hit the driver in the face. If it had been intended, only a trained marksman could have made the almost perfect form. There was a small entry wound, virtually in the middle of the drivers' forehead. The exit wound was larger and more destructive as the bullet slowed and split apart on its internal journey, creating a mess of blood, bone and brain on its way out.

Gerard turned the car off with a screwdriver that had already been forced into the ignition, trying to keep any remaining stomach contents where they were. He brushed the precariously balanced driver, who fell away from him, rolled off the seat and tumbled into the passenger footwell just as the car's exterior lights automatically dimmed. The silenced engine and extinguishing of the car lights immediately brought back the reality of the situation. There was the sound of movement a short distance away, and though it was likely to be the girl who had been dumped from the 4x4, it didn't mean there were no other dangers around. The fact also dawned on him that he was standing in the only lit area, completely unprotected, so he closed the car door to kill the remaining lights.

Nearly blind again Gerard stumbled down the incline toward his camp. He made a beeline to where he thought the gun had dropped and for once got lucky, picking the weapon up after accidentally kicking it. Now he had the pistol back, he sought out the source of the noise. He was right in thinking it came from the dumped girl, and after recovering the torch he turned it on to get a better view of her situation. It was readily apparent that only a countdown stood in the way of her becoming a threat, but this knowledge didn't help him with what he'd have to do to prevent that. Leaving her would only prolong the agony, never mind the damage she could cause when the disease finally took hold. Still, it was one thing shooting someone by accident or in the heat of the moment, but a completely different matter to be cold and calculating about the whole thing.

Leaving the girl for now, Gerard half hoped she would turn and make his choice simple. It was still a few hours until first light, but too risky to stay where he was any longer. He would only be waiting for the next attack coming out from the trees, or for some other unfortunate to stumble in on the bloodbath - and no one in their right mind would believe what had just unfolded and still think him innocent. Collecting the remainder of his kit, Gerard was glad of his earlier insistence to be ready for leaving. But instead of cycling off, he unceremoniously threw everything into the large boot of the 4x4. The gun was out and ready, and he constantly stopped, straining his hearing for anything unusual. The sounds from the young girl acted as an ongoing reminder of that unfinished business, and his hope she would turn didn't happen - he was going to have to do it the hard way.

Gerard took a jacket which lay crumpled up in the back of the car, and covered the girl's head. Levelling the gun he kept repeating the mantra "It's not a person, it's not a person." and was about to pull the trigger when music began to ring out from under the coat. She had a working mobile! He delved straight at the sound, pulling out the vibrating noisy phone and turned it off. He couldn't look at the display for any longer than it took to ensure he'd pressed the right buttons. Humanising her was not going to help the end solution.

He steeled himself again, then emptied his mind and pulled the trigger in one single move. He didn't look, or wait, but turned away and walked off like nothing had happened. He forced himself to concentrate on the road ahead, his next goal, the next meal, anything to deny the last hour`s existence. White noise and numbness whined through his skull again, like part of himself had been left in the trees with those other three souls. He hoped the numbness would always stay, so he would never have to face that time with any feeling.

14 A FINAL PUSH

Gerard opened all the windows to try to lessen the stench in the car. After a wretch-worthy removal of the driver, he made a half-hearted attempt to clean the inside of the cab. It had been a grisly task made worse with the looming threat of attack, but he couldn't leave it as it was. In the end the best he could manage was a wipe down of the windshield and seats to remove the worst of the visible gore, and anything left was covered with an old dog-haired blanket found in the boot.

It took a few attempts to start the car. The crash may have been an impact at slow speed, in a supposed off-road vehicle, but this was a fake townie jeep rather than a proper 4x4 and it hadn't taken the rear collision well. Once the car was pried from the trees, it limped along the fairly clear minor roads with an increasingly loud grinding noise coming from underneath. By the time Gerard arrived at Scotland`s boarders, nothing could be heard over the banging and vibrations echoing through the car's frame. It didn't take any great mechanical knowhow to tell this transport was on its way out, and he looked for somewhere to ditch the car. His timing couldn't have been better, as smoke and oil began belching from under the bonnet just as a suitable resting place was found.

He was being forced back onto two wheels again, and although the latest radio updates said not to travel he had no alternative. The reports advised things quickly changed for the worse since he'd left Manchester, and not only there. The army were being deployed all over the country to 'bolster over-stretched Police resources', and restrictions were beginning to be put into place. There were confirmed HarpIES cases reported in Europe, and with the spread getting worse the shipping ports and airports in the UK were all but closed. Gerard had left the city just in time, any later and he would have struggled to get out at all.

The sun was beginning to rise as he literally rolled the grinding car into an overgrown track which ran between two fallow fields. It was as good a place as any to dump the vehicle, secluded and judging by the road's overgrown state it was seldom travelled. He'd been tempted to just park up anywhere, but the legacy of his last stop and the bullet marked, blood soaked, and stolen car made him want to dispose of it properly - especially as his fingerprints and DNA were all over the interior. Sticking a rag in the petrol tank and running away would probably be the quickest and most effective solution to dispose of any evidence, but he didn't want to attract undue attention. A more controlled fire to burn out the interior seemed equally quick, and a less noticeable alternative, so Gerard took the emergency petrol can from the boot and liberally doused the inside of the car with fuel. Standing well back he lit a piece of blanket torn from his makeshift seating and threw the burning cloth back into the cab. He'd expected the seating to catch quickly, but the burning cloth hadn't even touched any surface of the interior before the flames erupted in a loud whoosh.

Gerard tried his best not to look back and check for signs of smoke as he quickly rode away with the mixed smell of singed hair and petrol in his nose. But the further he got, the more paranoid he became, and had to force down the internal voice which only wanted to go back and see if he was in the clear, but he didn't have the time. All he could do was hope that anything which hadn't burned would not lead back to him.

Eventually there was enough distance between him and the car for plausible denial, and he slackened his pace a little. At least he was in Scotland now, which was all well and good, but according to the maps and limited signage he was only close to Gretna. That left at least another hundred miles of winding hilly roads before he'd be near enough to the port at Stranraer for Motty to be in a position to pick him up.

Gerard felt a familiar buzz in his pocket, it was another text message. Shortly after going back onto two wheels he'd swapped the recovered phone's SIM card with his own. It was lucky the replacement mobile had nearly a full battery, for as soon as there was signal he started to receive multiple texts and voicemails from Motty and Bobby.

Before going any further he rang Motty. The call was opened with concerned anger, mostly due to the lack of his promised contact. With that moment aside they managed to organise a pickup point between them, or at least settle on the general area around Loch Ryan. Gerard wasn't the only one who'd been listening to the news, but Motty was more concerned with things happening seaward rather than on land. From what could be pieced together, even though the passenger ports were closed general shipping still wasn't blockaded, so he should be able to get over without being challenged. That didn't mean things wouldn't change, and Motty didn't fancy his chances running a small fishing boat against the Navy if things did turn. But for the moment success or failure was still within Gerard's control, he just had to push on and get to the pickup place as soon as possible.

Pulling in at the side of the road Gerard checked the message he'd just received. Some way behind he could hear the hum of a car engine, but paid it little attention as more than a few vehicles had now driven by since his disposal of the 4x4. Pushing off again, he looked behind in case the car was about to pass him on the narrow road, but it had stopped at the top of the hill. Straight away a hundred guilty thoughts flitted through his mind again. What were they doing? Had they seen him ditch the car earlier? Could they have followed him, and were now debated their own actions? Gerard beat his paranoia back down. Any comeback about the car disposal would have happened earlier, and he forced his gaze back to the direction he was travelling. There was plenty of reason to feel guilty and paranoid, but no one else knew about it and he'd already decided to never say anything about the gun or ill-fated rest stop to anyone.

In his peripheral Gerard heard the car clunk into gear and slowly set off. He expected the engine to accelerate as it approached him, but instead of the squeeze for space as there had been with previous vehicles there was only a delay and then a sudden impact on his backpack. Gerard tried to steer away from the car but could feel himself being pulled, and began to lose control. He swerved out to the right, then crashed heavily into a rusted wire fencing that ran each side of the road. He was dazed but not completely out of it, as his fall had been buffered by the overgrown grassy banks. He registered the car stopping, and began to get up to give a few choice words to the driver.

"Gi us that fuckin' gear pal!" A heavy accented Scottish voice shouted to him.

Gerard's heart dropped. For a second he thought they were only stopping to see if he was ok, but it wasn't the case - this was a robbery. He turned around to see if anyone else was on the road to help, but it was clear. They weren't that stupid, and had hung back to make sure of an uninterrupted opportunity.

"Cum on dickheed, or I'll fuckin' do ye! Nae cunt's cumin'." The guy shouted, pointing at Gerard with the business end of a baseball bat.

Pulling the pack from his back, Gerard made out as though he was going to throw the bag over, but instead ripped open the side pouch and drew out the gun.

"Why don't you fuck off instead?" Gerard responded, shakily levelling the revolver at his attacker.

There was a complete lack of reaction from the robber, who probably thought the gun was a fake never mind that Gerard would have the guts to use it. Before there was any chance for this opinion to be vocalised Gerard took aim at rear of the car and pulled the trigger. Firing a round near them should have been warning enough, but his inexperience made the gun jerk and the shot went in the rear window and back out again through the passenger side, smashing them both. Still, his point was proved, and ruled out the need for further retort. The attacker ducked behind the car, and was still trying to close his door as it sped off in a cloud of black-rubber filled smoke.

Progress was slower from then on, as Gerard stopped every time he was alone on the road with a car. The gun stayed as close to him now as he could get, in his inside jacket pocket. Luck had given him the edge once, maybe twice, but he wasn't going to rely on it again.

15 KILLING TIME

Gerard need not have worried about further 'hit and grab' incidents. He hadn't cycled another hour before the traffic thickened, and by the time he got anywhere near the port at Stranraer the roads were once more at a complete standstill.

Even though he had no expectation to find them, Gerard couldn't help but look for those who'd driven him off the road. His would-be robbers were either lucky, or knew the area well enough to have left the more popular routes before the queues formed, and probably just as well. While Gerard cycled anger blossomed in him. The fact this whole HarpIES thing was barely days old, and immediately the arseholes of society thought they had already taken over hit a deeper nerve in him than he knew existed. With the benefits of hindsight, Gerard internally re-enacted what he wished to have done at their encounter. He wanted to have left them bleeding by the side of the road, taken the car, and saved their next victims from a fate which could easily have been his. This line of thought sustained him as he warily cycled the winding last leg of his journey, but he had to let it go on entering the busy streets of Stranraer.

Like Gerard none of the other new arrivals in the town had paid any attention to the travel warnings, or news the ports were closed. From its outskirts, the roads were a gridlock of chaotic frightened looking families in overheating cars, loose groups of men talking and waiting on news of god knows what, and at least two separate army patrols equipped with automatic weapons and full riot gear.

Where desperate folks gather the opportunists also flock, and dodgy profiteering male vendors with savage looking oversized companions stood at the roadsides to sell water, hot food, and even sanitizer. The rates for everything were well beyond what you would think of as extortionate, but Gerard still stopped to part with £20 for two-quarter litre bottles of water. There was no barter or small talk, just pay the price and move on, and he did just that. There was nothing else for him or the other escapees in the town. The port was staying closed, and with that many frightened people gathering in one place, it was only a matter of time before something bad happened. Motty's boat would be able to get to there, but with so many patrols and stranded people about it wouldn't be safe for a clandestine pickup. He had to keep moving and find somewhere else.

Leaving Stranraer Gerard was again thankful he still had the bike as transport. Virtually nothing moved unless it was on two wheels or under its own steam, and even then progress was slow. He worked his way along the coast road, negotiating the six rolling miles to the next and final port at Cairnryan, all the time looking for somewhere to direct Motty's landing. The traffic situation here was equally as bad, if not worse than at Stranraer. Cairnryan was the last stop if you wanted to leave the country by boat, and for many people it was their final hope. Clueless about where to go or what to do next, some refused to go further and finally ended up parking at the side of the road or on any available waste ground. In places tents were already springing up, and plastic sheeting stretched between cars to make temporary shelter. This was already the beginnings of a shantytown, and quickly filling with refugees. It was also going to be Gerard's stop for a while, but he couldn't stay in the middle of everything. Rather than keeping with a possible volatile crowd, he made a final effort and pushed the bike to the top of a nearby hill which provided a relatively clear view over the Lough. He sat down without unpacking, and text Motty that he'd arrived in the area. Once he had confirmation that Motty was on the way, there would still be a few hours until Gerard had to make his final move. For now he could make use of the lull in activity.

The field where he sat was unused and overgrown, and left him hidden in high grass. But if the last couple of days had taught anything, it was to prepare for the worst no matter his expectation. A higher volume of people in the general area meant he could be stumbled upon, or already spied from some other vantage. Due to these circling thoughts the re-loaded gun never left his sight or side, and he was ready to lift his belongings at a moment's notice should anything began to get out of hand. He removed the tent and camping equipment from his pack, both items now surplus to requirements as there was no intention to stay any longer than it took Motty to make his way over the water.

Gerard tried to relax, but he kept picking up and staring at the mobile, hoping for a reply to his message that wouldn't come. He was dying to ring, but it was pointless. Text messaging was as good as things were going to get at present. Other than the two towns, this part of the country was still the Scottish highlands, and the usual poor quality or intermittent mobile signals were stretched to breaking point. He needed to be Zen about the whole thing, and have a little patience. He set the phone down again to wait on the text, and save the precious phone battery for when it may really be needed.

Not able to sleep, Gerard studied the map again to pass time. With the constantly growing numbers in Stranraer and Cairnryan, he had no chance of meeting up with Motty around either town without being spotted. He would have to take things further out into the surrounding greenbelt for any sort of clandestine rendezvous. That wasn't a great concern, as the normal population of the area was low enough so that he should be able to find somewhere discreet, especially as Motty's arrival would now be at night. On a calm day, the boat trip from Rathlin to here would be fairly easy. Both Motty and he had completed similar crossings before, but only on fishing trips, and in the best of conditions. For now Gerard could only hope Motty's experience would get him there, and send them both back to Rathlin unscathed and unnoticed.

The shrill alert from the text message made Gerard's heart and hands leap. The phone jumped in his grip like it had been oiled up. He'd picked up the mobile again to give it an intense staring, willing for the message, but it still caught him off guard. He saw the text was from Motty. It had to be the reply he'd been waiting for. Part of him didn't want to read it in case something new had happened, but at last his luck was turning.

'On my way, be close in 4hrs or so. You need to have a signal ready to guide me in. I'll light the yellow lamp here."

The ball was back in Gerard's court again, and up to him to find somewhere along the shoreline for a safe landing. The message revived him with the thought this nightmare may soon be ending. But he had to calm himself down, as rushing off without a fixed plan would only run him into trouble. He didn't feel hungry, but his body told its own story in a series of whining empty stomach noises. Rationing wasn't an issue any more, so he took the remaining food from the almost empty pack and turned on the gas stove. The least he could do for now was ensure starvation wasn't added to his list of things to worry about.

As the tinned food slowly cooked Gerard turned his attention to the real Loch Ryan, and cast his view up to where the water broke at its mouth into the Irish Sea. That's where he intended to go, out passed the Loch where the countryside took hold again. To have any chance of a successful uninterrupted pickup, the designated place for both signal and landing would need to be away from the sweeping lights, uniformed patrols, and milling frightened people who were waiting for the woman beside them to erupt in bloodlust frenzy.

The second batch of food was nearly ready when the small gas canister began to splutter, and then finally died out. Its demise didn't faze him, as even without it Gerard still now nursed a full stomach. His body cried out for sleep, but the brain had other ideas. Without realising it he'd close his eyes as fatigue took silent hold, then immediately the nightmares would resurface, shaking him awake again. Images he'd rather keep locked in the depths of his subconscious leapt up, breaking any respite. Broken, bloody faces, flashes in the dark combined with screams and cries for help. Gerard tried to clear his mind, but it was an impossible task. His guilt still bubbled too close to the surface, constantly probing for a way up, around or through to try and overwhelm and immobilise him. Resting was out of the question, so there was nothing else for it but to leave.

Gerard strapped on the much lighter pack, and pushed off on the bike. He'd left almost everything behind on the hilltop. The tent, stove, remaining food, anything that was bulky, heavy, or just not needed had been dumped. He got back on the road, and although the traffic was still slow, it wasn't as heavy as it had been earlier. After a winding three miles, the road that followed the Loch turned right and away from the shoreline. Fortunately there was a well-tended service road which ran off to the left, and then down to some buildings near the water. Gerard followed it, and after passing the buildings its tarmac covering abruptly turned to a packed clay surface. The road itself ended not a minute after, at which point the Scottish countryside began to take over again.

Dumping the bike in long grass, Gerard jumped a low wire fence that separated him from the shore. He walked along the water's edge for a few minutes, and quickly spotted a couple of potential landing places. There was still time to kill, so he went further on and shortly reached the perfect place. It was a small, natural inlet with a wide view of the Loch. The landing area was cut by the tides and time, and out of sight to both the main road and track he'd followed. Even if Motty couldn't immediately find the exact spot, all he needed to do was start at the far shore and make a bearing straight across the Loch mouth. If that wasn't enough Gerard would be waiting with a fire. First things first, he needed to tell Motty where to find him.

'Found a spot, straight across from the loch mouth. Keep a sharp eye. Signal fire will be burning, I'll keep look out for the yellow lamp."

For once there was reception on the phone, even if it was a flickering lone bar. Gerard still didn't call as it would waste the precious battery, so he sent the text. This time instead of the usual outbox pending status, the message sent straight away. All he had to do now was wait for the reply, and ensure a signal fire was ready at the proper time. He busied himself gathering dry driftwood, fallen branches and rubbish to make this happen.

On his rounds he saw a house, set back a little on a ridge behind him. It overlooked the water where his intended pickup was, and Gerard studied the building for signs of movement and life. At first the place seemed empty, but then he had to quickly duck back into cover when a figure walked from an outlying shed to the house. It was only then Gerard realised the fence he'd climbed over to get here was probably a boundary to someone's land. But it was too late to worry about it, events had already been put into action. He would just have to be as discreet as possible, in case anyone came sniffing around.

Backing away so couldn't be seen from the house, Gerard ensured there was enough wood and debris for a decent signal fire, and stashed the pile under some bushes so it wouldn`t be easily found. To prevent any unwanted attention he walked back to the road instead of loitering, and picked his bike up again along the way. He rode back towards Cairnryan a short distance, then turned out of the main traffic flow and onto the higher ground again.

Gerard turned left as the hill flattened out. He found himself on a deserted lane, and stopped at the top to catch his breath. He looked down the road, and saw two cars parked in an overgrown roadside layby. It was something he would normally dismiss, but his subconscious still sought out a car which had its rear window smashed - and now it found one. Recognition flashed though him, and instinctively he knew this was the car which knocked him down earlier, but he would need to get closer to be sure. His internal debate only lasted a second. Then he let curiosity get the better of him, and went to find out.

16 BACK TO THE FRAY

Stashing the bike and backpack in the verging towards the top of the lane, Gerard walked quietly towards the cars, looking around and listening for the missing occupants. The two vehicles were almost invisible between tall hedgerows that lined the road. He didn't recognise the car furthest from him, which had its doors locked and windows rolled up. This car was filled until nearly overflowing, but you could tell someone had taken hurried care packing its contents. These were the things the owners brought with them out of all their possessions, though the panic and rush to this dead end.

The car he'd been involved with earlier was a different scene. Most of the back seat, barring a small relatively clear corner section was filled with a rough and squashed jumble of plastic bags and holdalls. Gerard put a hand in through the broken back window, which had been smashed out completely since their last encounter, and looked in a couple of the nearest bags. Inside were expensively labeled clothes, all different sizes and sex. Intermingled with these were random electronics and other small personal items. Straight away he could see an iPod, a mini-DVD player, jewellery, mobile phones, a laptop computer, too many things in variety and number for only a couple of people. It didn't take a genius to figure these goods had been looted from those who were not able to defend themselves as well as Gerard had.

There was still no sign of either car's occupants, though Gerard thought the robbers wouldn't have strayed far from their previous form. He couldn't believe they would just park up and leave without taking advantage of such an easy target, so there had to be something he was missing. Leaving the cars he walked a little further down the lane, stopping at a heavy rusting gate that barred access to a field. He thought he could hear shouting, but the sound was intermittent and there was no telling if it was just noise carried on the wind from the road below. The land behind the gate looked as though it hadn't been worked in years, but new paths were carved through the long grass by recent foot traffic. Gerard's curiosity already had the better of him, so he climbed over the gate, trying and failing to keep silent as its old steel frame clanged and groaned under his weight and movement. He hunkered down on the other side and waited to see if his actions had attracted anyone, but no one came to investigate.

Following one of the recently made paths Gerard kept low, and quickly spied movement ahead of him. He veered off the track into untrodden grass, trying to create as much cover for himself as possible. He was approaching a makeshift camp which consisted of a single small domed tent. For a moment Gerard considered not going on. Getting involved was not keeping his prescribed low profile while waiting for the pick-up, but something about the whole scene ate at his conscience. Stealthily he kept moving towards the camp, and now began to hear excited shouting - then a woman's scream sealed the deal for him. The whole scene reeked of something unpleasant happening, and he couldn't leave until before finding out what they were up to.

Gerard took a wide circling route around the camp. He wanted to be sure he had accounted for everyone before getting much closer, but still needed to be near enough to see and hear what was happening. Starting his search where there was most movement, he found two men immediately. The first person he could have easily stood on, as he was face down on the ground, near to where a cooking fire still lightly smoldered. Gerard presumed this was the unfortunate companion of the girl heard before, and it looked as though the looters had dealt with him first to leave her unprotected. There was nothing he could do for him without moving into the open, and that would give away his presence too early, so he could only hope it was unconsciousness that kept the person floored rather than anything more permanent. The second man he spotted just outside the small dome tent. His movements were hidden from view as he faced into the open tent flap, so Gerard moved around further until he saw the robber was going through bags and removing anything deemed of value.

Out of nowhere the woman's screams broke the quiet day again, and this time Gerard was close enough to get a true bearing. He sneaked forward, peering through the grass to try to catch a glimpse of its source. Adrenalin was coursing through him already, the revolver held fast in his sweaty grip ever since he climbed over the gate. That quick dark anger flared up in him again as he stalked the group, melding with the adrenalin and carrying him on regardless of his own safety. Finally Gerard caught sight of those he looked for, and without further thought he rose from his crouched position while striding forward, gun levelled at the back of a male's head and shoulders which came quickly into view. As Gerard came up behind the man, he could see a woman struggling underneath him. The man was on his knees between her legs, pants down, showing his white arse as he thrust himself on her. The woman barely struggled anymore, the fight beat and bled out of her in a telling red stain that saturated and soaked into the dry ground around them both. Gerard aimed for the centre of the man's head, and pulled the trigger without pause. There was no mistake this time, no failure or miss-fire. The bullet created a small entry wound in the back of the head, but left the front in ruins. Chunks of bone and flesh struck the woman, followed closely by an almost headless torso that toppled lifelessly on top of her.

Gerard was committed now, and had no choice but to continue. He turned to face the tent scavenger who'd jumped up at the sound of the gunshot. The two looked at each other for a second, then Gerard raised the pistol again and began to walk toward him. He fired three shots in quick succession, all of them wildly missing, but this was enough to kick his target into action and the man rabbited. Gerard was in close now though, and had the time to stop, aim at the fleeing robber's back, and then squeeze the trigger. He knew the shot was on target even before its impact. Somehow it felt right, the gun an extension of his arm rather than some cumbersome heavy addition. He hit the runner square in the back, the impact making him fly forward and disappear into the grass. Gerard didn't check on him, there was no need with a strike like that, he was going nowhere. Instead he walked back to where the woman lay, and pulled the bloodied headless corpse off her. She didn't look good at all, and not only due to her recent brain shower. Her bruising had swollen excessively, leaving her face a battered mess. She needed serious medical attention, but that would be easier said than done. Gerard started to get up, but a glint in the grass a few steps away caught his attention as something bright reflected in the sun. It was the lens from a pair of glasses, and they belonged to a body that lain unnoticed to him. Gerard bent over the man, trying to find a pulse but there was no need. A thick trail of blood from a head wound, and an unblinking stare confirmed he was beyond any help.

For a moment the significance of the find didn't sink in. Maybe the couple were actually a triple? Then the car with the space in the back seat sprang to his mind - he'd been thinking about the wrong couple. Gerard whirled around to check the body by the fire, but it wasn't there and it was past time for epiphanies. He only realised something had hit him as his lights were already going out.

17 RUDE AWAKENING

There was a voice speaking. At first it was only sound, a distant hum of tone and flow, the words were meaningless with a barely conscious mind unable to put them into coherent form. Gerard's senses quickly began to reawaken, and he could feel the ground below him, warm and dry. In an instant there was smell and then the taste of blood. Pain exploded through him as he involuntarily twitched. Another new head injury sending an agonizing jolt down the length of his body, which nearly resulted in pulling him back down into the dark again. The thick male Scottish accent continued, either not seeing or just not acknowledging Gerard coming around.

"...came oot a naywher n started shootin'... I..I think thar deed... I dinny ken who..." The voice was quick, and held a frightened tone in his replies to the recipient on the other end of the line. This wasn't the sound of someone in control, but rather that of one being questioned.

The world slowly came into focus. The sickness and pain didn't leave Gerard, but the initial shock of consciousness loosened its overall grip a little. Opening his eyes he could see the partial profile of a body through the grass before him. A flash went off in his mind, the memory of being bent over someone, a third unseen man just before everything went black.

"You move 'n yer ded. You fuckin' hear me!"

Gerard froze at the outburst. He couldn't see who was talking, but erred on the side of caution. He waited a moment then tried to move his arms, but found they were bound behind his back.

"Nae fuckin' movin' cunt." The same voice shouted, anger replacing fear as its prominent timbre.

Gerard felt the kick to his stomach. The pain barely registering with him, but his body still automatically doubled up in reaction to it.

"Aye...aye e's coming 'roun..." Through the semi-conscious haze Gerard heard the voice continue, then it paused as the speaker continued to listen. "E'll be 'ere, but 'urry n...ello...ello."

The conversation ended abruptly, and the next moment Gerard was roughly grabbed by the shoulder and rolled over onto his back. The movement caused white pain to ripple through him, greying out his vision. Gerard forced himself to breathe and managed to focus again. He was greeted with a snarling, pale face staring back. His captor was knelt beside him, with a split lip, and there was swelling and dark bruising around his eyes.

"I dinny ken yer problem pal, but ur oot o order wey this." The pistol barrel poked roughly into Gerard's face, and was then removed to point over to where the 'third man' lay. "Yer bird's man - that wer'n accident. He shouldn'y came at Dexy shoutin' the odds." The man pointed at his own face. "Look at wat the cunt Dexy did tae me, n` wer friends. Just oer strange fanny to. She wer jus a bit o fun – nae fuckin' wurth dying oer. No matter, I'm no gettin' the blame fer this. The bruther of thon hedless cunt's oan his wey, an e's gunna rip you a newun' - maybe a few."

Gerard's captor lent back out of view, and then stood up. Gerard slowly moved to keep him in eye line.

"You stay ther' ye bam, or ye'll git anar smack..." The voice trailed off slightly as he spoke, the next sentence said more to himself. "...n I'll sort mesel fore they cunts dae."

With those final words Gerard was left alone again. No matter what the situation his captor's greed still rose to the top of the totem, and he walked a few paces away to the couple's tent, then busied himself taking the cream of what had already been pawed over, stuffing the items into his pockets.

Gerard knew he couldn't wait for another opportunity, and immediately began to struggle against the wrist bindings whilst trying his best to keep movement and noise to a minimum. The knot didn't seem like it was something he could untie without seeing, but whatever had been used to bind him had a little give in it. After a subdued struggle, which still nearly caused him to black out again with the effort, he was able to get a hand free. He lay still again and waited to see if his movement was noticed. He could hear something in the grass a little from him, and rose a little to see what it was. His view was obscured with the grass, but it looked like the decapitated torso of Dexy was moving, and it wasn't only Gerard that had heard it.

"I to'l ye tae stay...What tae fuck!" Gerard's captor saw him still on the ground, when he realised the noises were coming from elsewhere - then he saw Dexy moving.

"That fuckin' bitch's still gan on. Git oot 'ere ye fucker." He spoke to the back of the re-animated corpse. "Fuksake, git oot." Now he bent down, and grabbed a flailing hand which had appeared from underneath, pulling it hard toward him.

The woman slid out a little from under the other body, but instead of the expected hysterics and confusion from a battered and raped woman she tightened her grip and pulled him towards her, biting hard into his forearm. With a scream and heavy spray of blood the man tried to pull his arm back, but she wasn't letting go. Remembering the gun in his other hand he fired a missing shot before trying to aim, then the gun click, click, clicked as he kept pulling the trigger. It was no misfire, all the rounds in the pistol had been used. Now staggering back he dropped the weapon, and instead tried to pry the woman's locked mouth from his arm. He slipped on the uneven bloody ground, giving the Harpie her chance. She straddled him, attacking with her mouth and hands, while his screams became a high-pitched squeal of fear and pain. He shouted for Gerard to help, but that wasn't going to happen. He had already set off in a stumbling run, his focus only on keeping upright. It was a battle he had already lost, as the darkness of unconsciousness crowded in around him again.

18 THROUGH THE FIELDS

Gerard felt like he was flying. Instinctively he knew his legs and arms would still be pumping automatically below him, but his mind had already left the physical plain behind. His body slowly toppled with its captain no longer at the helm, and Gerard's spirit soared upwards into clean, clear blue skies - soon to be lost among the gathering clouds and ether.

Again it seemed only moments before when he fell in the long grass with the Sun above him, but as Gerard regained consciousness the gold tinged dark blue of post-sunset, lengthening shadows, and gathering rain clouds told him he'd drifted for longer. In the distance, further into the field there was shouting. The voices were close, but they were not on top of him - yet. He managed to collect himself enough to sit up, despite his body's protests that it still wanted to cling to the cooling dry ground. He looked back in the direction where the calls came from. At least three people were spread out across the field, noticeable by their torch lights whose beams swept the area in different directions.

"Dexy...Johno...Marty..." The calls repeated themselves in different tones and intervals, as the friends of those he and the Harpie dealt with searched the field.

There was no return to their shouts, and Gerard knew there wouldn't be unless the last of the robbers had somehow managed to overwhelm his role-reversing attacker. This was the first and only time Gerard hoped there were HarpIES around, and they would be attracted by the shouting. But for the moment he could only pray the search party's focus would stay in a different direction than he needed to go, for something told him if he was caught things were not going to end well.

Shakily he got to his feet, and began to walk as quietly as possible back towards the road. He tried to stay off the fresh tracks so he'd be less visible, but it was difficult. Where his steps earlier in the day were almost silent, now everything was magnified in the relative hush of dusk, and with each footfall he expected someone to shine their light in his direction.

'Beep, beep' the phone in his pocket sounded. Gerard grabbed the mobile, trying to silence it, but already it was too late.

"What the...Hello, hello?" A disembodied voice rang out, and Gerard saw a shadow detach itself from the deeper background darkness at the entrance to the field.

His only exit was back over the creaking gate, but a quiet getaway wasn't going to happen with someone blocking the way. Gerard was at odds with what to do next. He might be able to rush the gate and leave from the same place he'd come in, but he didn't feel in any condition fight his way out. Then his decision was made for him, as with no response the lookout began to shout.

"Hey! Over here. Someone`s over here!"

Gerard was left with no choice but to flee along the hedge line. He chanced a look behind, and sure enough the thin torch beams were bouncing back across the field in his direction. Stealth didn't matter now, and he took off as fast as his shaking legs would carry him. He kept close to the hedge, trying to keep his silhouette from being spotted along the otherwise open horizon.

Suddenly a large gap appeared in the hedge, and Gerard ran passed another open gate before realising what it was, wasting precious seconds doubling back. There was no one immediately behind him, and he made use of the new exit that led up to a farmhouse. Gerard sprinted through the concreted forecourt, his footsteps echoing on the hard surface that set the farm's dogs off who started to bark from the closed outhouses. Even the dumbest of those searching would automatically be drawn by the noise, but at least the dogs were locked inside and not out snapping around his heels to slow him further.

Reaching the road Gerard could only assume pursuit was close behind. The reinvigorated barking of the dogs told him he was correct, but he still chose to run back to the original entry point and collect his things. The speed of the bike would serve him better than trying to run back to the shore, but even disregarding transport he wasn't leaving his bag next to a multiple murder scene with an abundance of incriminating evidence neatly packaged inside. He approached the turning where everything was stashed, just as two high beam lights came flying along the road in front of him. Gerard launched himself into the hedging verge, knocking his breath out and snagged his clothes on a rusted barbed-wire fence hidden in the foliage. He lay as flat and dead still as possible, even after the car screeched to a halt just after it passed him. He filled with terror as the vehicle stopped. They'd saw him, and he was lying there like a trussed turkey. His mind squealed to try and pull free, its base flight reaction trying to overrule everything, but he managed to contain himself. Then the voices of two people spoke up.

"Anythin'?"

"Naw, fuck all. You?"

"Naw, we'll gan other way, n bac' again. They cunts better nae be takin the pish."

Gerard heard a car door open and close again, then the engine revved and the vehicle took off in a screech of burning rubber. He tried to calm himself down.

'They haven't seen you.' He repeated to himself. 'Just get up - Get up!'

Gerard untangled himself from the fencing, ripping his clothes from the wire and then managed to stand. He began to look for his possessions, and for a moment thought they had already been found, but then he spied the handlebar of the bike glinting in the dim light. He grabbed the bag, pulled his bike out, and then unsteadily began peddling off in the direction of the loch.

19 BACK TO THE EDGE

His return journey to the shore may have all been downhill, but to Gerard it still seemed to take an eternity to get back to the water. Even though he'd left the immediate search area, every car, or new light skimming the horizon made him think his pursuers were upon him again. Until he reached the slip road to the shore he hadn't thought about the phone, or trying to contact Motty. Now he pulled the mobile out, and turned it on as he stumbled across the overgrown ground beyond the end of the road. A series of beeps from messages began to come through in quick succession again, all of them it seemed from Motty.

'Nearly there. Running the boat dark, make sure you are ready.'

'I'm here! At the mouth. Where ru? Text or ring me!'

There were other texts, those being the glanced detail of the first two, but he had saw enough. Gerard was late for the pickup, and could only hope Motty managed to stay his ground and had not turned away. Blindly he ran the length of the bank, stumbling to the cove where the signal firewood was stashed. The time for building this was long gone, but even if there had been time it was now rain heavily, and it instantly soaked him along with everything else in the area.

Gerard checked the phone again. The smallest of reception signals was still flickering on the handset, so he tried his luck and hit the dial button. Instantly the low battery notification beeped, and he thought the phone had turned off, but moments later a crackling voice came through.

"Hello...Where the fuck are you?" Motty's voice broke up in places, rising and fading with the reception so some words were lost, but his angry tone still came through with crystal clarity.

"I'm here, come get me now!"

"I've been waiting dickhead. I would`ve left if it wasn't your arse hanging about. I'll light it up again."

The crackling on the line increased in volume, then there was a disconnected beep and the phone went silent. Gerard didn't know if he'd been hung up on, if the signal had just failed, or the phone had just died, but the mobile had served its purpose. Motty's signal light was the only direction he would need, and once seen there was nothing left but to go for it. Gerard opened his rucksack, and placed his few remaining items into a plastic shopping bag. He blew the bag up, tying a knot in the top to keep it buoyant and the contents dry, then wrapped the handles around his wrist.

It took all Gerard's self-control not to set off at the first flickering light he spotted on the water, but he had to be positive it was Motty and not just a random marker or reflection. Motty flashed the yellow light again, and though the signal was further out than he`d anticipated, there was no choice but to begin moving out into the water. One thing he hadn't taken into account was the tide, and this had gone out while things were happening at the campsite. Even with its shallow bottom, Motty wouldn't have been able to get the boat any closer to shore without possibility of being grounded on the mud. No matter, there could be no further delays and he began to wade out into the water.

Even though it was mid-summer the temperature of the water still took his breath away. It froze his core almost instantly, and the rain only serving to compound the issue. The walk from the shore was fairly simple at first with his initial steps on a graveled shoreline, but soon he began to get bogged down by sediment. Each step sunk him deeper into the bed, and the effort to keep bringing his legs up quickly took his strength. As he reached the beginning of the shipping channel, the Lough floor sloped sharply downwards. The extra depth fueled the size of the waves, with their increased size and renewed force almost knocking him from his feet. As a final check before fully committing, Gerard looked to see if he was still in line with the signal light from the boat. He saw the bobbing yellow light dead ahead, and with a final effort heaved himself up from the mud, leaving his shoes behind which the suction of the bed claimed for themselves.

As soon as his feet left the floor, Gerard found his fight was only beginning. He didn't class himself as a strong swimmer, but living on a small island he'd swam in the sea plenty and wasn't a beginner. Still, the current caught him with unexpected force, and he was swept away from the boat, immediately forcing him to start swimming against the current to try and stay in his current position. The loch was choppier, and the current much stronger than anticipated. With the drag against him, the waves tried to overwhelm with each clash, and the bag causing further interference. Gerard tread water, catching his breath while trying to find where he now was in relation to the boat. As he bobbed around, the waves still got larger and more ferocious with each repetition. One moment he just about staying afloat, and the next he had to claw his way back to the surface. Coughing and spluttering he got back up again. His lungs burned with swallowed water as he gulped down air in the ebb of the now towering waves.

Looking around there was now no sign of the boat or signal, his bearings were mixed up under the water and sense of direction lost. He tried to shout, but for his efforts only received further mouthfuls of water. Another large wave washed over him, sending him back under. He tried to swim back up, but his own weight and failing strength kept him under. Instead of panic, he felt surprisingly calm, but his mind was now fogged. Abstractly he thought there would be pain, and though he could feel the water filling his lungs it was as though it happened to someone else. He was connected, but only peripherally like filling a glass of water from the tap. Tiredness overwhelmed him, and in some small corner of his mind he could hear Mandy calling again. Gerard sank further down, his thoughts sporadic. He was back in bed, the last few days melting into nothingness.

In cold comfort he slipped away into the soft embrace of the water.

20 EPILOGUE

Three months had passed since the first HarpIES case was reported in England. Fortified by its water boarders and distance from mainland Northern Ireland, the island of Rathlin suffered little in comparison to the world's wider population. The paranoid islanders had been swift to respond to the crisis, closing their small harbour to traffic and terminating the scheduled ferry route that would normally still be in constant transit at the latter part of the year. Pre-HarpIES the island had already been mostly self-sustaining, and only the requirement of fuel or new machinery were the outside drawbacks to the community. If it hadn't been for the lack of summer tourists and a scarcity of diesel, the island would probably have trundled on as it always did.

Today was a little different, and the adult residents were gathered in the community centre. This was a building which until the crisis usually served as a welcome centre for visitors to the island's floundering bird sanctuary. In times before the 'HarpIES problem' began and ended every meeting, topics raised in the centre rarely rose above the political hot potato of Puffin nesting habits, or a lack of lighting on the main street. Today's meeting followed the same meandering path, and there was no reason to think it wasn't going to end on the focal point every debate had since the 'outbreak' was quantified. That debate was 'who would be taking the risk to go to the quarantined mainland for supplies, and how would the island's people be sure the returnees were not infected?' Or more commonly 'who would be suckered into going, and how much segregation could be inflicted upon any returning heroes without the remaining islanders feeling too guilty'.

Dermott Moran shot a fleeting sideways glance at his brother Gerard, who to the casual observer seemed to be staring out the window and not listening to the meeting at all. This wasn't entirely true, but both he and Gerard where pretty sure the next run was going to land on their plate, and wished the lazy witch hunt would just get to the point. Those in the building were exiles here by choice, no matter if they were born on the island or had at some point purposely moved there. Under normal circumstances they didn't like going to the mainland, and now that returning may mean not getting back at all, or you could qualify for an indefinite home quarantine, people were using every favour not to be named on the next outward boat.

This was the first meeting Gerard attended since his timely reappearance back on Rathlin, and he was only there due to a formal invite. His suspicions were not unduly raised, as since the outbreak the brothers were recipients of an unspoken shunning from the other residents. Fortunately this suited the pair fine, as it gave Gerard time to recover from his return journey, and partial drowning. The night Dermott found him in Lough Ryan had only been through luck, blind panic, and an unusual visual marker of a blown-up plastic carrier bag Gerard had fortunately tied around his wrist. He was neither conscious nor breathing when Motty dragged him on board the boat, and though Dermott brought him back coughing and spluttering on the fowl smelling deck, he'd not been the same person since. Dermott wasn't sure if he'd ever get the full story of the journey, or even if he wanted to know the details. Sometimes things were best left to scab over and heal, rather than worrying the wound until it festered and infected further. Dermott was in a minority of one with his opinion of leaving things alone, and as there'd been a couple of HarpIES cases on the island with no confirmed source to pin it on fingers pointed in Gerard's direction. His invite to the meeting only meant those concerns were being overshadowed by something larger, and that would only be one thing - they were going to get dumped on for the Ireland trip.

For a while no one noticed the increasingly loud rotor sounds above the debate, but they soon became a distraction. Just as people began looking out the windows, the door of the centre burst open and one of the island's few children came running in.

"The Army's coming, there's a helicopter and everything!"

The meeting instantly ended, with the residents trooping out of the community centre whilst scanning the sky. As the helicopter hovered in its search to find somewhere suitable to land its noise drowned out everything else, and Gerard had to tap Dermott on the shoulder to attract his attention, pointing out to sea. The helicopter was only the forerunner of the visitors, rather than their entirety. They had brought friends with them, and the bows of the ships broke through the light waves with speed and purpose, heading directly towards the island.

The helicopter slowly descended onto a patch of scrubland close to the harbour. As soon as its wheels touched earth two men in army fatigues jumped out from the rear cabin, and hunching over to avoid being decapitated by the spinning main rotor they jogged towards the crowd.

"Who's in charge here?" The snippy bark came from an upper-class sounding English officer who looked as though he`d just been through basic training, rather than being any kind of veteran.

The small crowd looked around at each other. No one had formally taken charge, but eventually eyes began to shift to Shaun McCandless, who while not holding any official capacity always had an opinion owing to the land he controlled and money his family infested in the area. McCandless strode through to the front of the crowd and stopped before the arrivals, trying and failing miserably to keep a smug look from his face at being branded 'in charge'.

"Shaun McCandless, I'm..." McCandless stuck his hand out in greeting, but the act of welcome was bluntly ignored and instead the officer firmly planted a thick rolled sheaf of paper into his open palm.

"Everyone listen up, this concerns all of you." With his baton passed over, the officer ignored McCandless and addressed the crowd as a whole. "Subject to conditions set out in the Military Lands Act circa 1900, all viable land not in use for food production is to be held in care by the Ministry Of Defence..."

A murmur of disbelief echoed its way through the crowd, but the officer ignored the grumbling and continued without breaking his pace.

"Any parties affected will be financially compensated, dependant on size, location and present use of the land. But let me stress, any requisitioned property falls under the jurisdiction of the MOD. Unauthorized access to those areas will be treated as trespassing on military ground, and subject to the same laws. Please direct any queries to your representative or liaison, who has been provided with the relevant documents. Individuals will be informed in due course regarding any valid claims..."

The residents of Rathlin had a hundred and one questions, but for the moment these were forgotten as they watched not the military or navy leaving the boats, but women, laden down with bags and boxes. All of them hoping this destination would finally prove to be a safe haven.

ABOUT THE AUTHOR

Trevor Samuel Nicholl was born in Coleraine, Northern Ireland. He currently lives in Manchester, England with his wife Debbie, and two spoilt cats.

The HarpIES was his first novella and he is currently working on a new novel, Last night at The End.

www.ingramcontent.com/pod-product-compliance
Lightning Source LLC
Chambersburg PA
CBHW051237070726
47594CB00013B/409